THE GIRL FROM KILKENNY

A gripping thriller, full of suspense

PETE BRASSETT

THE
BOOK
FOLKS

Paperback published by The Book Folks

London, 2017

© Pete Brassett

This book is a work of fiction. Names, characters, businesses, organizations, places and events are either the product of the author's imagination or are used fictitiously. Any resemblance to actual persons, living or dead, events or locales is entirely coincidental. The spelling is British English.

ISBN 978-1-5205-9902-1

www.thebookfolks.com

If you can keep your head
when all around you are losing theirs,
you're probably the one with the knife.

PROLOGUE

No doubt you're familiar with the phrase: 'Empty vessels make the loudest noise'. True enough, so it is, and generally speaking, they're the gobshites you can ignore, always mouthing off, always bragging or complaining about little or nothing. No, it's the quiet ones you have to watch for, the quiet fella who keeps himself to himself, just goes about his business, buried deep in the undergrowth of life, troubling no-one, just watching and working and listening.

And simmering. Slowly simmering until a flat battery, a red light or a final demand tips him over the edge and sends him spiralling out of control, at which point he perpetrates some heinous crime and then, for some reason, for some strange reason, we all act like we didn't see it coming. 'But he was so nice,' we say. 'A bit of a loner,' we say. Then, what do we do? I'll tell you, we shake our heads in sympathy, raise a glass to toast his passing and move on. Within a month, all but forgotten, the only time you'll hear his name is when someone's had a skinful of ale and a drop too much of the old whiskey.

So you'd have thought, especially around here, that we'd keep an eye on each other, you know, make sure that we're all okay. I mean, we're all in the same boat, right? And let's face it, 'tis a struggle, so, from sun up til sun down, and when times are hard, life becomes a worry, and then the stress sets in. It's easy to spot, if you know what to look for. I've seen it meself, from Ballinacurra up the road, down to Kinsale and on to Cork. Men without a decent coat to keep out the cold, or enough change for a drop of whiskey, let alone the luxury of putting something other than a plateful of feckin' spuds on the table. And if the weather blights the crop, and they can't even do that, that's when you see the desperation in their eyes. The hunger, the anxiety. But what can you do? Trouble is, as soon as you ask someone if they're alright, if they need a hand, like, the old pride takes over. 'Ah, sure, 'tis nothing,' they say, 'I'll be fine.'

Take Dermot for example, a lovely fella, not yet fifty, worked the land, man and boy. The cattle were his pride and joy. Charolais they were, fine looking herd, eighty strong. Then the BSE came and they were slaughtered. He lost the lot. Six thousand guineas on the bull alone with not a hint of compensation from anyone. Not even the feckin' government. Ah, sure, he could've sold the tractor but then, how was he to plough the field? He could've got a loan on the house but then, how was he to pay it back? He could even have robbed the Post Office, but the fact is he was so well liked by everyone in the village, they'd have given him the money tied up with a black, velvet band. And, of course, he could have asked for help, but did he?

No. Instead, he robbed his family. He robbed them of a father and a husband. Hung himself, so he did, in the woods, up the way there. We thought he'd taken himself off, a wee break, like, to clear his head. It took four days to find him, by which time he wasn't pleasant to behold. Selfish? Maybe. Thing is, old Dermot, he had some life assurance, some savings and a pension too, so, maybe not so selfish after all. See, when he took his own life, he knew exactly what he was doing and it was probably the most selfless, most generous thing he'd ever done. His family have never had to want for anything ever since. Except a father and a husband, that is.

Then, there's Nancy. Dear Nancy. At least she didn't hang herself. She just went away. Faded into the night like a dying ember and disappeared without a trace. Strange thing is, she took nothing with her except the clothes that she was standing in. According to Brendan, everything's still there, just as she left it, her shoes and boots, her dresses, even her make-up and her hairbrush. They're not the kind of things you leave behind if you're not coming back.

Now, I'd be lying if I said I wasn't surprised. Truth be known, it made me bones go cold. It was out of character, see, not like her at all. The family was everything to her and she was strong, a fighter. Defeat was not in her vocabulary. At least, not until the stress took a hold. It came like a cancer, slowly spreading, creeping silently, invading her entire being til it became so rife that, I'm guessing, she felt, I don't know, trapped. And if you feel like that, then you only have two options open to you: fight or flight. Animal instinct so it is. And that's why I was surprised. She chose flight.

As a daughter-in-law, Brendan couldn't have wished for anyone nicer, always going on about her, so he was. Probably because she made Fearghus so happy. She was the quiet type, unassuming and generous to a fault. She never, ever put herself first. When she cooked the supper, she was the last to sit, and if there wasn't enough, she went without. Why, of late she'd even walk to town so she could use the bus fare to buy Fearghus a bottle of beer. There was nothing to her. A slip of a thing she was, but she was tough, sure, she could lift a bale or carry a ewe as good as any man.

3

She never spoke of her past, not that it mattered. I'm not even sure where she came from. There was talk of Laois, I think, but then again, Kilkenny rings a bell too, so who knows? All I do know is that the day she breezed into town, young Fearghus came alive, and when he proposed she went weak at the knees and wept for days. It was like they were separated at birth. Nine years they were together, nine years, joined at the hip like Siamese twins. They worked their fingers to the bone, no hired help, no farm hands, just the two of them. So it was hard. Very hard. Ah, sure, Brendan, bless him, he helped when he could, but let's face it, there's only so much an old fella can do except make sure there's a coal on the fire and tea in the flask.

They were arable, mainly, barley and maize, but they had enough sheep to keep the mint sauce coming too. Then, they had a bad year. It happens. Everyone suffered, the whole county. But, you dust yourself down and just get on with it. That's the way it is. Thing is, that bad year was followed by another, and then a third, and there was no-one to blame but the weather. At least they had the sheep, and sheep, as you know, are tougher than me own hobnail boots. They'll take the wind and the rain, the snow and sleet, the freezing nights and the blistering days. Sure, they'll cope with almost anything, unless, of course, it's something like the Scrapie.

The vet and the inspector said there was a chance it could've come from Dermot's herd but they couldn't prove it, and, just like Dermot's lot, the flock had to go. Destroyed they were. 'Twas a sorry sight to see, watching them being loaded up and carted away, especially so soon after lambing, too. That's when they took to arguing, Fearghus and Nancy, and who can blame them? Mainly about money it was, just the odd tiff, now and then, like any other married couple I suppose. Only, the tiffs grew longer and the shouting grew louder and there was nothing anyone, not even Brendan, could do to help.

4

August 23rd. I remember it well. The weather was foul, had been for days. Fearghus had started breeding pigs by then, 'twas the only livestock they could rear after the Scrapie thing. But Nancy had already lost interest. She thought they were a waste of money, money that could've been spent putting food on the table. Anyway, that morning, they'd argued. About what, I'll never know, but it was enough to rile her, enough to make her so angry that she took herself off and that was the last we saw of her. It was their anniversary too. And that made it worse. Fearghus had a gift for her, a small andalusite ring. He'd been carrying it around for weeks and was going to surprise her with it that evening. That evening that never came.

The police did though. Came knocking on their door and scared the shite out of him. Brendan too. A couple of days later, a few posters went up here and there, and the peelers made an appeal on the television. Then, I'm sad to say, folk lost interest and Nancy faded into obscurity. Fearghus, the poor lad, riddled with guilt, so he was, blamed himself. And, as for Brendan, well, it's enough to make you weep. He's half the man he ever was, if that. Lonely, withdrawn, never goes out. Just sits about with the worries of the world on those fragile shoulders.

Stress. 'Tis a terrible thing, stress. It can break a man, so it can. Break him in two.

CHAPTER 1

Nancy had much to be grateful for, not least her husband, for it was Fearghus McBride who'd given her a sense of purpose, a direction in life. It was Fearghus who'd loved her for who she was, despite the mood swings and inexplicable silences that would last for days. It was Fearghus who'd taught her how to smile. It was Fearghus who'd given her hope for the future. As she gazed out across the lush, green field where the sheep used to graze and the lambs used to bleat, she realised he'd given her something else, too. Something she hadn't counted on. Despair.

She toyed with the ring on her finger. Eighteen carats of white gold. Diamond inlay. It had a value, but no longer the sentimental kind, a few hundred, maybe, perhaps a grand. Enough to tide her over for a couple of months. She could sell it, but not in Kinsale, not even Cork. Eyebrows would be raised, questions would be asked, rumours would start to spread. She'd have to go elsewhere, somewhere farther afield, somewhere where she wouldn't be recognised. If only Fearghus had kept up the premiums on the livestock insurance she wouldn't have to stoop to selling her jewellery. If only he'd put in a claim for compensation for the loss of the sheep, then perhaps they wouldn't be living hand to mouth. If only he'd faced up to his responsibilities. If only.

* * *

'Sorry,' she whispered, as she stroked his head and returned to the task at hand, 'I'm so sorry.' She cleared her throat, picked up the cleaver and brought it down hard. It slammed through his leg, severing it just above the knee. There was no blood to speak of, just a sad, sorry look of betrayal in his big, innocent eyes. She rolled him onto his back, hesitated as she crossed herself then brought the cleaver down for a final time, grimacing as his head parted company with the body. She wiped her dry, cracked lips with the back of her hand and, holding him gently across the belly, picked up the paring knife. The blade sliced silently through his skin as she drew the knife the length of his torso. Close to tears in the fading light, she slipped her fingers beneath the wound and, to the sound of a silk sheet being slowly torn in two, gently teased the skin from the flesh.

She froze as the front door slammed, cocked her head and listened. Muffled footsteps shuffled down the hall. She drew a breath, a long, deep breath and held it. The veins in her arm bulged as she gripped the knife. The kitchen door creaked open. Fearghus, silhouetted by the light from the hall, stood and scowled in disgust.

'Rabbit?' he barked. 'For feck's sake, Nancy, can we not eat something else?'

Nancy sighed, traced an index finger along the buck's naked stomach and sliced it open before reaching in and yanking the intestines free. A single tear clung to her eye.

'It's all we have,' she sniffed. 'Just be grateful. This fella gave his life for you, just so's you can fill your belly.'

'What?'

7

'One minute he's bounding round the field, happy as Larry, not a care in the world, next thing, he's in the feckin' snare. It's not right.'

'But…'

'Can you not at least shoot them, or borrow a ferret? Winding up dead with a length of wire round your neck is no way to go, it's too feckin' painful. 'Tis torture, so it is.'

Fearghus kept his distance. There were times, he'd learned from experience, when it was wiser to say little and do nothing.

'Are you okay?' he asked softly.

Nancy paused, opened her mouth as if to speak, then thought the better of it. The last thing she wanted was another argument, another fight, another spat over something that was out of their hands.

'You're filthy,' she said, forcing a smile. 'You've mud everywhere. Why don't you take yourself off and have a shower. There's plenty of water, so.'

'In a bit,' said Fearghus, 'I want to look at the paperwork first.'

Nancy clenched her teeth and swallowed hard, forcing back the months of frustration which threatened to spew at the slightest provocation. It was obvious that remaining in the same room, breathing the same air and sharing the same meal with the man she'd married was becoming increasingly difficult. She was suffocating.

'Christ, I need a drink,' she mumbled to herself.

'What's that?'

'A drink,' she yelled, 'I need a feckin' drink!'

Fearghus, accustomed as he was to what he described as 'irrational and unfounded hormonal outbursts', smiled gently and beckoned his wife to the table.

'Come so,' he said, setting down a clay bottle, 'it's your lucky day. Poteen, from me Da, he'll be along soon.'

Nancy took two tumblers from the wall cabinet, sat down and filled the glasses with a generous dose of the toxic potato juice as Fearghus randomly waded through a mound of papers, bills and final demands.

'So, how's it looking?' asked Nancy, coughing as the whiskey burned her throat.

'Well,' said Fearghus, 'looks like we're down to our last million. We'll have to let the servants go.'

'Be serious.'

'Not great. We still owe for the feed and the concentrates even though we've no sheep left. And the oil's gone up, just like everything else.'

'Do we need the oil?' asked Nancy, as if she cared.

'Sure, no, not really. We'll just freeze to death when the bastard cold sets in.'

'Not a bad idea,' she said, gazing at the ceiling, her thoughts wandering. 'Maybe we should change, start anew, go dairy. Maybe.'

'Now, that's a grand idea,' said Fearghus. 'All we have to do is build a milking parlour, get some cattle and wait for the supermarkets to pay us a penny a pint for our trouble.'

'Just a suggestion. I could milk them. That would save on the cost.'

'You, with a fistful of udders. Are you mad?'

'Pity. Quite fancied one of those milkmaid outfits.'

Fearghus grinned. As usual, the storm clouds were passing and Nancy was softening, helped in no small way by the poteen. She downed her glass, wheezed, and filled it up again.

'Okay. Let's forget the livestock,' she said. 'Why not crop the whole lot?'

'And what do you suggest we plant? Mangoes? Cotton, maybe?'

'Kestrel. They're hardy enough, and…'

'Spuds? That's what got this country into trouble in the first place.'

'Well, we can't use the field for grazing anymore, not til we get the all clear. We can't go on like this, Fearghus, we have to do something or I'll end up feckin' killing you. So help me, I'll…'

Nancy jumped as the door flew open.

'Now, now, what's all this, then?' said Brendan. 'I can hear you two down the hall.'

'Brendan, didn't hear you come in,' said Nancy.

'Not surprised.'

'Hello, Da,' said Fearghus. 'Still raining?'

'A few spots, nothing to worry about,' said Brendan. 'Now, I'll take a glass of that, if you don't mind,' he said, nodding towards the poteen.

Nancy managed a smile for her father-in-law as he slumped in the armchair, his boots caked in mud, his jacket drenched. Raindrops gathered on the peak of his cap and fell, one by one, to his lap.

'Sure, I don't know what you see in it,' said Nancy, as she passed him a glass of whiskey. 'All that walking, day in, day out.'

'You should try it, lass. Come a walk with me next time. All that clean air, good for the soul, so it is.'

'Good, my arse,' she said. 'Where'd you go?'

'The river,' said Brendan. 'Over by Whitecastle.'

'Whitecastle?' said Fearghus. 'But that's feckin' miles away.'

'I know. But it's where I have to go.'

'Still looking for those coins, Brendan?' asked Nancy.

'I am. And I've two more, now.'

'So, how many's that, in total?'

'Six, I think.'

Nancy shook her head and sighed with a puff of the cheeks. Fearghus and Brendan watched in silence as she returned to the sink, jointed the rabbit and tossed it into a casserole. Fearghus caught her eye. Her vacant gaze troubled him.

'I'm away, so,' she said, wiping her hands on her jumper.

'What?' said Fearghus. 'In this weather? Where will you be going at this time…'

'Out. Just out.'

'Why?' said Fearghus. 'Will you not just sit with us and…'

'No. I can't listen to you talking about the farm anymore, Fearghus. I can't take it. It's our livelihood and all you do is talk, talk, talk. Just do something about it. Stop talking and feckin' do something.'

'Ah, come on, Nancy, there's no need for…'

'Let her go,' said Brendan as the door closed behind her. 'Let her go. You may have been married nine years, son, but you've still a lot to learn. She'll be fine, soon enough, she'll be fine.'

Nancy knew the lane like the back of her hand. So well in fact, she could walk it blindfolded. With the low cloud, no moonlight, and a fine, persistent drizzle, she may as well have been. She had no intention of going to town. There was nowhere in particular she wanted to visit, no-one she wanted to see, her feet simply led her there.

Forty minutes later she arrived in Market Square, stood for a moment and shivered, as though she was surprised to be there. The only sign of life came from The Grey Hound. With its misted windows and soft, yellow light, it looked warm and inviting. She drove her hands into her pockets and fumbled for any loose change. She could tell, simply by the feel of the coins, that she had enough, just enough, for a half pint of Murphy's.

'Nancy!' said Aiden. 'Looking lovely as ever!'

Embarrassed, Nancy coyly tucked a tress of sodden, raven black hair behind her ear and smiled.

'Stop now,' she said softly.

'If it's Fearghus you're after, I've not seen him.'

'No, I was just, I just fancied…'

She paused and locked eyes with a stranger seated at the bar. He was young, at least ten years younger than herself. Dressed in an Argyll sweater, beige chinos and college loafers, he looked as though he'd stepped from the pages of a vintage clothing catalogue. '*Another feckin' tourist,*' she thought. He grinned to reveal a set of cosmetically enhanced teeth and raised his glass.

'He's right you know, you do look lovely,' he said, with a predatory glint in his eye.

The accent grated on her. It could have been West Coast, it could have been the Deep South or even New York, she didn't know and she didn't care. It was American and that was enough to raise her hackles.

'Don't tell me,' she said with disdain, 'your great, great, grandfather was called Seamus O'Flaherty, he was born in Kinsale to a family of leprechauns, and you've come to find his grave.'

The stranger smirked, took a sip of whiskey, and slowly set his glass atop the bar.

'Actually, he was called Antonio Balducci, he was born in Naples, lived on the Via Nardones, and he's buried in the Cimitero di Poggioreale.'

'Oh.'

'I'm here for the golf. My pals are out back, in the snug.'

Aiden glanced at Nancy and winked.

'Drink?' asked the stranger, 'what'll you have?'

Nancy hesitated, shuffled nervously from foot to foot and turned for the door.

'No, I'd best be off,' she said.

'Aw, come on,' he said as he pulled a wallet from his back pocket. 'Have one on me. No hard feelings, huh? I'm Josh, Josh Balducci. One hundred percent Italian-American. Not an ounce of Irish, guaranteed.'

Nancy caught sight of the stranger's wallet. She had never seen so many banknotes crammed together in such a small place before. So many banknotes with a '50' printed in the top right hand corner. She blinked, rapidly, as though afflicted by a tic and nibbled the nail on her right index finger.

'Paddy's,' she mumbled, keeping her distance. 'Paddy's, a large one. Thanks.'

'Well,' said Josh. 'I know your name's Nancy, and you don't look like a golfer, so I assume you live here, right?'

Nancy glared at him contemptuously.

'Christ, you're clever,' she said. 'You should be a detective.'

'Too dangerous. I like to play safe. Accountants are safe.'

'Sláinte,' she said, knocking back the whiskey. 'I have to go.'

'So soon? But we've only just met, have another, I promise I won't bite.'

'Sorry.'

'Tomorrow, then?'

She hesitated.

'No, No,' she said. 'Maybe.'

Flustered, she bowed her head and left.

CHAPTER 2

The clock chimed eleven as Fearghus, elbows on table, cradled his mug of tea and watched his father dip a small, metal disc into a bowl of soapy water.

'Doesn't look like a coin, Da, just a bit of rusty old metal,' he said softly.

'There's no rust, lad, it's gold, and gold, as you know, doesn't rust. All the same, 'tis a bit like alchemy, I suppose. Pass me that toothbrush. Now, watch.'

Brendan gently scrubbed the coin, taking care not to mark the surface, until all the silt and grime had been washed away.

'Where's Nancy?' he asked. 'Gone shopping?'

'No, she's in bed, so. Sleeping.'

'Sleeping?' said Brendan. 'At this hour? What time did she get in?'

'No idea, I was out for the count.'

'That's not like her. I fear for that girl, you need to keep an eye on her. There, take a look at that.' Brendan held the coin aloft and passed to his son.

'I will, Da, don't you worry. Jesus, it's like new. What is it?' asked Fearghus.

'A gold crown.'

Fearghus squinted as he scrutinised the inscription.

'1650,' he said. 'That's old, so. It says here, 'Commonwealth of England'.

'That's right. You see, after the Civil War, once that fella Cromwell had gotten rid of Charles I, he governed the whole of England, Scotland and Ireland and that was known The Commonwealth.'

'Right, so? Is it worth much?'

'Enough to scare me,' said Brendan.

'How scared?'

'Very.'

'Then why not sell it?' asked Fearghus.

'Because they'll ask me where I found it and then they'll all come looking. I want to be sure I have them all first, or as many as I can get. Then our troubles will be over.'

'How many are there?'

'Can't say for sure. Thirty, forty, fifty, maybe,' said Brendan.

'Fifty! How do you know?'

'Fintan Fitzgerald.'

'Who?' said Fearghus. 'Never heard of him.'

'You have so, do you not remember? When you were a babbie. And then some, your Mammy, God rest her soul, used to tell you the tale to get you off to sleep.'

'What tale? You mean, like a fairy story?'

'Yes, if you believe that fairy stories are based on fact,' said Brendan.

'Remind me.'

Brendan took a deep breath before delivering the well-rehearsed soliloquy.

'Three hundred and fifty years ago, in the hills above Carrigleigh, lived a fella called Fintan. Fintan Oisin Colm Fitzgerald.'

'That's a heck of name,' said Fearghus.

'The Fintan was a heck of a man. A man of few words, the fortunate few who did get to speak with him came away, enlightened. Troubled by nothing, he had what you might call, an inner peace. He led a simple life. By day he watched his sheep and fished for slumbering trout. By night, he prayed beneath the stars. Some thought he was mad, a demented recluse, others, well, others saw him differently.'

'Differently?' said Fearghus. 'How so?'

'They thought he was, divine. A saint, no less. A messenger of God sent to guide them, protect them. Sent to save them from Cromwell and his marauding Roundheads.'

'And?'

'Well, Cromwell heard about the Fintan, see. He grew nervous, worried that a man of God might rise up and lead a rebellion. He was petrified he'd be defeated and so, one fine morning, he sent a dozen troops to seek him out and there, on the banks of the Toon, Fintan Fitzgerald was arrested.

'They took him to the castle at Carrigadrohid, chained him to the wall and left him hanging there without so much as a drop to drink. That night, Cromwell himself paid him a visit. They stood, face to face, by the light of the moon. The air was damp and musty, water trickled down the walls, rats played at their feet.

'Cromwell stared at Fintan with scared, steely eyes. He longed to hear him beg for mercy but not a word crossed his lips. Frustrated, Cromwell declared that hanging was too good for Fintan…'

'Well, that's good, isn't it?'

'…instead, he would be crucified at dawn.'

'What?! Are you feckin' joking me? Crucified?' said Fearghus.

'I kid you not. That was the price of his faith.'

'But he got away, right? I mean, he wasn't…'

'He got away, lad, that, he did. To this day, no-one knows how the Fintan slipped his shackles, but slip them he did. Shielded by the night, he dropped from the tower onto a cart below, took up the reins and raced to freedom, south towards the Bandon, on to Whitecastle and beyond.'

'And the gold?' whispered Fearghus, enthralled. 'What about the gold, Da?'

Brendan paused, took a sip of tea and, as if exhausted, leaned back and clasped his hands behind his head.

'Ah, the gold,' he said. 'The gold was in the cart. Cromwell's cart. Legend has it that the Fintan buried it by the banks of the river but neither he nor the gold was ever seen again.'

'You mean, until now, that is.'

'Until now,' agreed Brendan.

'Jesus, Da, did no-one else think to look for it?' asked Fearghus.

'There's plenty have tried, and just as many failed.'

'Then, how come, how come you…'

'I knew where to look. See, everyone's been looking on the banks of the river.'

'But you said that's where the gold…'

'And it was, three hundred and fifty years ago. Have you not heard of a thing called erosion? What used to be the bank is now the river bed and that part of the river is tidal, so I can only get down there twice a day, and not for long at that.'

'You're feckin' clever for an old man.'

'I know.'

'So, where did you hear about this? I mean, the gold and this Fintan fella?'

'Your Mammy. She was born up the way, there. She's the one who convinced me it was true.'

'But how did you know it was buried at Whitecastle?'

'Maps. We used to spend hours looking at old maps. See, the only thing we had to go on was part of a rhyme she learned as a child:

*Where the river babbles softly
and the ripples makes no sound,*

where the bracken and the ferns
shed teardrops to the ground,
where the Bandon weaves its way
in search of space to rest,
lies the treasure trove of Cromwell
and the Roundheads' last bequest.

Nancy stood in the doorway, her arms folded, her brow furrowed. She gazed at the sink, piled high with dirty dishes, the casserole blackened with the burnt remnants of the rabbit stew, the worktop strewn with toasted crumbs.

'Treasure trove, my arse,' she said. 'Glad to see you're on the case Fearghus. If only there were more like you, this country would be up on its feet in no time. Don't worry about the dishes, your skivvy'll clean them up.'

'Ah, she wakes!' quipped Fearghus. 'You must've been late, did you sleep alright?'

Brendan kicked his son under the table as a subtle reminder of when to shut up.

'I slept well enough. It's the waking that bothers me.'

Brendan stood, took the bowl to sink and tipped away the murky dregs of the river water.

'Sit yourself down, lass, I'll get you a tea. Will you take a slice of toast?'

'I will, Brendan, thanks,' she said as she sat, preferring not to look her husband in the eye. 'So, what's the plan, Fearghus? I assume you have one that doesn't involve nursery rhymes?'

Fearghus smiled. There was something intangible about his wife's mood swings that endeared her to him even more.

'I do, that,' he said.

'Let me guess, you know a fella selling magic beans.'

'Almost.'

'Impress me,' Nancy challenged him.

'Well, to start with, I'm going to get the top field ready for an autumn crop of barley. The weather's improving, so we need to get that in. Then I've to see a fella up in Clouracaun. He's going to take the concentrates off our hands, for a price, of course, and then, I was thinking of, wait for it... pigs.'

'Pigs?' said Nancy. 'You'll feel at home, so.'

Fearghus grinned and swilled back the last of his tea.

'I was thinking Landrace, they're good breeders. One sow to start with and a couple of dozen weaners, til we get going, like. We could rear them free-range and, who knows, in a year or two, maybe we could go organic.'

Nancy stared at the table.

'Are you mad?' she asked.

'How's that?'

'There's nothing but pigs around here. Thousands of them. The whole of Cork is nothing but a bacon butty factory. You've too much competition, it'll never work.'

'That's why I thought free-range, then organic. It'll give us the edge.'

'Have you forgotten how long it takes to get organic certification? Give me strength!'

'You know something, Nancy?' said Fearghus. 'If there's one thing I admire about you, it's your enthusiasm. You've such a positive outlook on things. See you tonight.'

Brendan passed Nancy a mug of tea and a slice of buttered toast. As Fearghus left the room he sat beside her at the table.

'He's doing his best, lass,' he whispered reassuringly. 'Doesn't help if you chew his face off every time he suggests something.'

'I know,' sighed Nancy. 'It's just that... it's just that things don't seem to be getting any better, Brendan, and I don't know how much longer I can put up with this.'

'You have to give it time, lass. Nothing...'

'Time? What about the money? How's he going to pay for the pigs? Or the feckin' barley for that matter? Anything we make on them will go straight out the window and we have little enough as it is. Can you remember the last time we ate something that wasn't hopping round that field? Or sat together with a bottle of wine instead of a flagon of feckin' potato juice? Sorry, Brendan, I'm just, I'm just…'

'What's up, lass? You know you can…'

Nancy threw her head back, sighed and rapped the table in frustration.

'It's nothing, just a headache,' she muttered.

'I'll fetch you an aspirin.'

'No, you're okay, Brendan. Feels like a migraine coming on. I'm away to get something stronger.'

'What about your tea? And your toast?'

* * *

'It's me, Josh! Last night, remember? The Grey Hound?'

Nancy, somewhat perplexed, regarded him with a look of confusion, her vacant eyes staring blankly into his while her hands fumbled furiously with a carton of tablets.

'Need a hand with that?' asked Josh.

'No!' she said, surprised by the encounter. 'No, thanks. I…, I forgot to get some water, I have to go.'

'I'll get you some, come on, that's my hotel, right across the street.'

Nancy looked back to the pharmacy then across to the hotel.

'The Blue Haven?' she remarked. 'Alright for some.'

The bar was deserted save for the staff who busied themselves polishing glasses and flicking imaginary flecks of dust from the tablecloths.

'Guess we're early,' said Josh, as chivalrously pulling back a chair by the fireplace. 'But it is lunchtime. Let's eat, my treat.'

Nancy shuffled nervously in her seat.

'Just a glass of water, please. I'm fine, so.'

'Sure? I'm always hungry, me. Must have something to do with my metabolism.'

Nancy raised her eyes to the ceiling.

'Maybe you have worms,' she said.

The waiter, swooping like a kestrel diving for a kill, landed at their table and whipped an order book from his breast pocket with a theatrical flourish.

'What'll it be, folks?' he asked. 'Just drinks or can I get you something from the menu?'

'I'll have the steak sandwich,' said Josh. 'Nancy?'

She shook her head. Hungry though she was, she would rather starve than dine out on the charity of a brash American.

'Well, okay, just a steak sandwich then, and a glass of water for the lady.'

'Coming right up.'

'So, no golf, then?' Nancy asked, teetering on the brink of boredom.

'One day on, one day off. Today is my day off,' said Josh.

'What about your friends? Don't you have to visit some old ruins or something?'

'They're grown men, they can look after themselves. I enjoy my own company.'

'Somebody has to,' said Nancy, as she ripped the top off the carton.

'Headache?'

'Something like that.'

'May I?' asked Josh, picking up the pack. 'Tryptizol? That's a new one on me, is it...'

'It's for...' Nancy stopped abruptly. 'It's for... headaches. Any more questions?'

Josh raised his hands defensively and smiled.

'I have an inquisitive nature,' he said wryly.

'You mean you're nosey.'

'Are you always this hostile to strangers?'

'Only those I like,' said Nancy.

Josh spread a napkin across his lap as his sandwich arrived.

'You really are something else,' he said, grinning. 'I don't think I've ever met anyone quite so... How can I put this? Rude. But, I forgive you.'

'Why?'

''Cos you're so darn pretty.'

Nancy, popping a pill from the foil strip, blushed profusely. She watched as Josh demolished the sandwich in a couple of minutes flat. Forgetting herself, she raised her right hand and pointed half-heartedly towards his mouth.

'You've sauce, on your... on your chin. There,' she flicked her finger.

Josh wiped it away and sat back.

'Thanks,' he said. 'So, what shall we do now?'

'I'm sorry?'

'Well, if you're not too busy, I thought you might like to show me round.'

Nancy hesitated, caught between the flirtatious flattery and the irrefutable knowledge that even sitting opposite the man was wrong.

'I'm not a feckin' tour guide,' she said. 'I'm busy. I should go.'

'Shame,' said Josh. 'Well, if you hold on for just a moment, I'll walk with you, at least to the top of the street. I just have to, er, you know.'

He gestured to the waiter.

'Here, you take this,' he said, tossing his wallet on the table. 'Back in a flash.'

Nancy glanced furtively around the bar before allowing he eyes to settle on the fat, brown, leather wallet. She ran a finger over the monogrammed initials embossed on the surface and jumped as the waiter startled her with the bill. She snatched a twenty and placed it on the tray. Left alone, she quickly flicked through the remaining notes, counting as she did so: 50, 100, 150, 200, 250. She stopped at 600 and surreptitiously slipped a fifty into her coat pocket.

'All done?' said Josh, pulling on his jacket.

'Yes, I… I gave the fella a twenty. He'll come with the change, so.'

'It's okay, we'll call it a tip. Shall we go?'

The twenty second walk to the top of Pearce Street should have been ample time for Josh to blurt out an invitation to join him for drinks that evening, but his infatuation caused him to dither. Nancy, guessing intuitively what was coming, grew impatient, mumbled a curt goodbye and disappeared into the crowds.

* * *

'Pinch me,' said Brendan, as he pulled off his boots.

'What?' said Fearghus.

'Can you not smell that? I want to be sure I'm not dreaming.'

The unmistakeable smell of steak and onions, searing and sizzling in an open pan, attacked their senses as they entered the kitchen.

'Is it me birthday?' asked Brendan.

'Did we win the lotto?' asked Fearghus.

Nancy looked up and smirked as they eyed the table suspiciously.

'Wine?' said Fearghus. 'There's wine too! How did we afford this, Nancy?'

'Ask no questions,' she said. 'Ask no questions.'

A 'thank you' might have been nice. An offer to do the dishes would have been even nicer. She'd have refused, of course, but nonetheless, it would have made a difference. Instead, she was left to clean the kitchen on her own. To wash the dishes and scrub the pans, while Fearghus and his father, slumped on the sofa, sipped their wine and called for her to join them.

'At last!' said Fearghus, patting the sofa. 'Come, sit with me, you must be worn out.'

'No thanks,' said Nancy. 'It wouldn't be right, servants mixing with the master and all. Drink your wine, I'm away so.'

'Again? Where on earth are you going now, will you not rest a while?'

'I promised Brigid I'd drop by. She's missing Dermot so, something rotten.'

'Ah, well, that's understandable, we all do,' said Fearghus. 'It's not been long. Tell you what, I'll come with you, cheer her up.'

'You will not. Girls' stuff, so it is. Don't wait up.'

Fearghus studied his glass and spoke quietly without looking up.

'Do you think she's alright, Da?' he asked. 'I mean, she seems a bit distant, like. I'm worried…'

'So you should be,' said Brendan. 'It's healthy to worry, so. Keeps you on your toes.'

'I know, I know, but… I just get the feeling she's, she's…'

'Listen, Nancy loves you and don't you forget it. Things are tough, that's all, for all of us. She's a fine lass who just filled your belly with a half a cow and a bottle of wine. Now, do you really think she'd do that if she didn't care?'

'No, I suppose not. I just wonder how she paid for it.'

'Probably slept with the butcher.'

* * *

Nancy wasn't worried, nor did she harbour any guilt, just a tinge of nervous excitement, the kind associated with risk, the risk of getting caught. Besides, she wasn't doing anything wrong, even if it didn't feel entirely right. If Fearghus could share a pint with whomever he chose, without fear of retribution, then so could she.

She checked her reflection in the shop opposite The Grey Hound, hoping the American would pass by. The waxed cotton jacket was frayed around the collar, her boots had seen better days and her hair may have been better tied back, but she would have to do.

A small group of men, chatting loudly and dressed for a night on the tiles, ambled up the street. She stepped forward as they approached the pub then quickly turned away, a subtle gesture intended to get her noticed. Josh ushered the group inside, muttered something about forgetting his phone, and skipped over to Nancy. He looked different. Dressed in a lounge suit, his hair carefully coiffed, his square jaw clean-shaven, he looked almost acceptable.

'Hey! This is a pleasant surprise,' he said warmly, smiling as though it were a first date. 'Come on, I'll buy you a drink.'

'What?' said Nancy, feigning surprise at their chance encounter. 'Are you not being a wee bit presumptuous? What the hell makes you think I want a drink? With you?'

'Well, I just thought…'

The smug expression coating his face riled her.

'Alright,' she said, 'but I can't go in there, everyone will start talking. Anyway, it looks like you've other plans, at a feckin' casino or something.'

'No plans, we just had dinner, that's all.'

'Oh.'

'So, how about the hotel, then, we could go there, or another bar maybe?'

Nancy hesitated.

'It'll have to be the hotel, I'll get recognised anywhere else, but I can't go through reception, not dressed like this.'

'Like what? You look beautiful.'

Nancy scowled as though she'd been insulted then dropped her head and allowed herself a subtle smirk.

'Sorry, didn't realise compliments were off the agenda,' said Josh. 'Come on, we can slip in through the restaurant, no-one will see us.'

Nancy hovered by the entrance and peered through the glass doors. It was packed.

'Okay?' asked Josh.

'I don't know, they're all dressed up. There might be someone I…'

'So what's the problem? It's not as if…'

'It's night time and I'm going into a hotel with a fella that's not me feckin' husband, that's the problem.'

'Okay,' said Josh with a shrug of the shoulders. 'Point taken. Look, if you'd rather forget it, I won't mind, really, but I don't know where else we can go. Well, apart from my room.'

Nancy said nothing. Instead she turned her head and stared blankly at the menu hanging by the door, as if deciding whether the restaurant's offering matched her appetite, then glanced down the street and back again.

'Right, so, but we go straight up, no hanging around or nothing.'

The room surprised her, it was a far cry from those she was familiar with, those with cheap, flat-pack furniture, a bed draped in a brown blanket and a TV bolted to the wall. It was homely, furnished in a Regency style and large enough to accommodate a king size bed, two armchairs, a solid oak wardrobe and a dresser, not to mention a writing desk with complimentary stationery. It was a shame the occupant didn't treat it with the respect she thought it deserved, its grandeur tarnished by the copious amount of clothes strewn about the floor, the bedside tables littered with personal effects and the pile of dirty laundry stacked against the dresser.

'How long have you been here?' she asked incredulously.

'Four days,' said Josh.

'And how long are you staying?'

'Two weeks.'

'You better tip the feckin' maid.'

Josh smiled, removed his jacket and tossed it on the chair.

'So, how about that drink?' he asked. 'What shall we have? Champagne?'

'What? Don't be an arse,' said Nancy. 'Wine or something.'

'Okay, I'll scoot down and get it. Room service takes an age.'

'Don't ask for glasses,' said Nancy. 'They'll know you've company.'

The view from the second floor was nothing remarkable. It was still Pearce Street, just a different angle. She closed the curtains, hung his coat on a hanger, cleared the clothes off the floor and stashed the laundry in the bathroom. She stood, hands in pockets and perused the debris scattered atop the bedside table: travel clock, house keys, nail scissors, tour guide, pocket knife, passport, tissues, half an apple and a pack of golf tees. She resisted the urge to sweep it all into the drawer and turned her attention to the dresser: comb, hair gel, moisturiser, aftershave, deodorant. It was too much. She was about to tidy up, when Josh returned.

'Hope this will do,' he said, holding a bottle aloft.

'Paddy's. That's grand, so.'

'I remembered, from the pub, you asked for it by name.'

'I did, that. So, will we use the teacups, or the glasses in the bathroom?'

'Teacups. Be like a speakeasy.'

'If you say so,' said Nancy.

Josh dimmed the lights as she slipped off her jacket and hung it on the door. She was slight, petite even. Wearing a checked shirt and denim jeans, she would not, he concluded, look out of place on a ranch, nor for that matter, the veranda back home. He moved towards her and handed her a cup. Nancy looked up, craning her neck, realising only then just how tall he really was. He was so close she could smell his aftershave.

'So, then,' she said, making an attempt at conversation, 'Where're you from?'

'New York,' said Josh proudly.

Nancy sipped her whiskey and groaned.

'New York? Oh, don't tell me,' she said 'You're one of those feckin' Wall Street hotshots, with a big fancy car, smoking big cigars and…'

'Actually, no. For the record, I don't smoke, I drive a '92 pick-up and I'm not a corporate guy, I'm a CPA. My clients are local businessmen, store-owners, mechanics, that kind of thing.'

'In New York? I thought it was all skyscrapers and…'

'Only the city, which, incidentally, I can't stand. I live in a village called Larchmont, out of town, very quaint. It's kinda like Kinsale.'

'Is that so?' said Nancy, her enthusiasm waning.

'Sure, it's right on the coast, too. Here, I'll show you a picture.'

Josh opened his wallet and leafed through its contents.

'That's odd.' He said, frowning.

Nancy, assuming he'd noticed a fifty was missing, drained her cup and looked nervously around the room.

'It's missing.'

'Sorry? What is? What's missing?' she said, staring at the carpet.

'The photograph. I could have sworn…'

'Ah, don't you go worrying yourself, now,' she said. 'I'm really not interested.'

Josh, confounded by her attitude, placed his wallet on the dresser while she did her best to avoid his gaze. A stony silence filled the air as he topped up their drinks.

'What is it with you?' he asked quietly. 'Is it something I said or do you just hate Americans?'

'Hate Americans?' she said sarcastically, accepting the invitation to battle. 'Now, why would I hate Americans? I have a lot to thank them for. Sure, I wouldn't be here if it wasn't for them.'

'What do you mean?'

She paused.

'Doesn't matter. I should go.'

Josh placed a hand under her chin and gently lifted her head until they made eye contact.

'You wouldn't be here unless you wanted something,' he whispered menacingly.

'I don't know what you mean,' she said, turning away.

Josh noticed her eyes settle on the dresser.

'Oh, I get it,' he growled, reaching for his wallet. 'I should've guessed. Okay, how much? Two hundred? Three?'

'What?'

'How much? For, you know...'

Nancy glared in astonishment, her blood boiling.

'What? What did you say?' she snarled. 'You think I'm a feckin' whore? Is that it? You think I'm some kind of feckin' prostitute?'

'No, no, I mean...'

She threw the whiskey in his face and tossed the cup aside.

'That's it,' she said. 'I'm away, so. I have to go.'

Josh blocked her path and grabbed her by the shoulders.

'Hey!' he said with sudden gentleness. 'Hey, calm down. I'm sorry, really. I am. I don't know why I... It was a stupid thing to say, a misunderstanding. I was out of order.'

Nancy slowly raised her eyes to his. He pulled her close and kissed her, his breath tainted with whiskey. She didn't respond, her top lip curled in disgust as she taunted him:

'That the best you can do?' she whispered, mockingly.

Josh, his ego unaccustomed to ridicule, pushed her violently to the bed, straddled her waist and pinned her arms behind her head. He leaned forward until his mouth was a hair's breadth from hers.

'I'll show you my best,' he said threateningly.

Nancy sneered.

'Lay another finger on me and the whole feckin' town'll be out to lynch you.'

He leaned forward and kissed her again.

'I dare you,' she said, goading him on. 'I feckin' dare you.'

Josh jumped up and hastily stripped to his shorts. His frustration, fuelled by the whiskey, soon turned to anger. Nancy, rather than struggle, lay motionless and detached as he unbuttoned her shirt, wrenched her jeans to her knees and sat astride her. He stared into her deep, green, lifeless eyes and frowned, perplexed at how someone so alluring, so pretty, could be so cold.

'Go on, then,' she whispered through clenched teeth, 'feckin' do it!'

She stared at the ceiling, as vapid as a tailor's dummy as he slathered over her neck, drooling and slurping like an eight-year-old devouring an ice lolly. His breathing grew heavy and loud as she teased him with her hips, gently rocking, back and forth, groaning with all the enthusiasm of a hooker on a date. Josh mumbled profanities under his breath as she feigned arousal. Whimpering softly, like a puppy in distress, she placed one hand on the back of his head and lashed out with the other, knocking everything from the bedside table. Everything except the pocket knife.

'Well?' she whispered impatiently.

Josh frowned, furious that his infallible foreplay had been interrupted. His lip trembled with rage. Nancy pulled his hair and moaned with indifference as he fumbled clumsily with her knickers.

'Okay,' he hissed, as if squaring up to a bare knuckle fight. 'Okay, bitch, let's see how you like this, eh? Let's see how you…'

He stopped, abruptly, surprised at the unwelcome intrusion which disturbed his concentration. Bewildered, he gazed down at her in a state of utter confusion. It took a few seconds for his brain to determine whether the sensation of the cold, carbon steel slowly piercing the flesh in the small of his back was pleasurable or, as it transpired, excruciatingly painful, by which time it was too late.

'How does that feel?' she whispered. 'Does that feckin' turn you on?'

His expression turned to panic as she drove the knife deep into his back and yanked it forward, smiling as the blade glided effortlessly through the tissue, bumping and jarring against the vertebrae, severing the spinal nerves as it went. A look of terror washed over his face as his right leg suddenly gave way and he realised, as his ardour waned, that he no longer had control of his bowels.

'Come on!' she panted. 'I'm waiting!'

Paralysed with more than fear, he winced and moaned as torturous cramps riddled his abdomen, the crippling pain a sign that his internal organs were shutting down, first the pancreas, then the kidneys, then the liver. She drew the knife again, deeper, harder, this time with a sawing motion, swiftly slicing the length of his spine. One by one, his muscles, unable to respond, turned flaccid and lax. He opened his mouth as if to scream but all he could muster was a sharp, desperate, intake of breath.

Nancy groaned with the effort as she tugged the knife up between his shoulder blades when he suddenly gasped and expelled a muted, agonising sigh. His blood pressure soared, his pupils dilated and his head, dripping with sweat, thumped and pounded as a thousand migraines bounced around his skull. His face flushed and his skin burned with an intolerable, blistering heat while his heart raced erratically, uncontrollably, trying desperately to maintain a rhythm. Then, as if accepting defeat, it suddenly slowed to nothing more than a pathetic pulse until all communication with the brain was lost. His arms collapsed without warning and he slumped in a heap, almost crushing her diminutive frame. She listened to him wheeze as his lungs breathed their last.

'That's a great feckin' knife,' she muttered, as she plunged it deep into his neck and released her grip.

He gurgled, softly, like a contented baby, suffocating as his throat filled with spittle and blood. She could feel the faint, final murmuring of his heart pumping feebly against her chest. She held her breath and waited, and waited, until finally, it stopped. Using her middle finger, she traced the length of the wound and relished the warm, wet, sticky feel of the canal she'd carved along his spine.

Her mind a blank, she lay perfectly still and savoured the silence. A minute passed, then five, then twenty. She turned to face Josh. She felt no remorse, had no desire to cover her tracks and wasn't in any particular hurry to leave. Instead she regarded the clean-cut, square-jawed, misogynistic tourist with contempt and sneered. Eventually, as if waking from a heavy sleep, she yawned, stretched, and wriggled out from beneath the rapidly cooling carcass and washed her hands before making herself decent. She glanced around the room. Apart from the clothes she was standing in, there was nothing for her to leave behind and little worth taking. Except the whiskey. And the wallet. The wallet crammed with credit cards and notes the owner could no longer use, notes that deserved to be liberated as recompense for his abhorrent behaviour.

'Three hundred?' she whispered to herself. 'I'm not that feckin' cheap.'

CHAPTER 3

'Da.'

'Morning Fearghus. Sleep well?'

'No, not really. Has Nancy been through?'

'Nancy? Sure, no, why?' replied Brendan.

'She didn't come home last night.'

'Did she not? Fair play to her, she deserves a night out.'

'It's not like her, Da, I'm worried,' said Fearghus.

'Good. So you should be. Did you phone Brigid?'

'Brigid? What for?'

Brendan raised his eyes.

'Because, you eejit, that's where she went. Did it not cross your mind that she may have stopped over?'

Brendan filled a flask with steaming, sweet tea, pulled on his mud-encrusted boots and sniffed with disgust as he caught a whiff of his overcoat, still reeking of damp. Fearghus returned, glowing with relief.

'You were right, Da,' he said. 'She's with Brigid, sleeping, so she is. I'll go fetch her.'

'You will not,' said Brendan, sternly. 'Leave her be, she'll come when she's ready. Poor lass is stressed enough as it is without you looking over her shoulder.'

'What do you mean, stressed? Now, why on earth would Nancy be stressed?'

'Have you been eating some of Dermot's beef? Why do you think? Money, the farm, the future, your future, shall I go on?'

Fearghus sat like a berated child and sighed.

'I never realised.'

Brendan gave his son a reassuring pat on the shoulder as he made for the door.

'Just leave her be. Least said, soonest mended. I'm away now.'

'Where you going? Back to Whitecastle?'

'I am, that.'

'Would you rather not help with the ploughing?'

'I would not. I think you could use some time on your own.'

It was late. Fearghus gazed across the empty fields, blinded by the setting sun. It was quiet, he thought, too quiet. There were no sausages sizzling in the pan, no pots bubbling on the hob, and no Nancy. No arguments, no shouting and no awkward silences. Just the uncomfortable feeling of being left alone. He rummaged through the cupboards in search of something to eat. Baked beans, tinned sardines, more beans, a packet of corn flakes and a tin of tuna. He jumped as Brendan breezed through the door.

'Two more!' he cried. 'Two more, could've been three if the feckin' tide hadn't turned.'

Fearghus's mind was elsewhere.

'All we have is beans and a half a loaf,' he said. 'That do you?'

'Grand,' said Brendan, as he hung his coat and kicked off his boots. 'Why the face? Something wrong?'

'Have you not heard?'

'Heard? Heard what, now? Did you lose another million?'

'Very funny. I saw Aiden, down the lane, there. He said some tourist got killed last night, American fella, at the hotel.'

'Is that so?' said Brendan, shaking his head. ''Tis a tragedy for these parts, that's for sure. What was it? Another bar brawl?'

'Don't think so, unless he was followed. Dead in his bed, so they say.'

'That'll teach him to complain about the room service, they don't take to criticism, those people.'

'Da…'

'Ah, they're just exaggerating, so, you know what it's like, Chinese whispers and all. He probably died in his sleep, heart attack or something. Or choked on a feckin' peanut.'

Fearghus paused, can opener in hand.

'They say, they say he was sliced open, like a side of beef, cut from top to bottom,'

'What?'

'All along his back, they say you could see…'

'That's quite enough, I'll not need the detail.'

'Apparently the Garda had to leave, threw up, so he did.'

Brendan crossed himself and took the half empty bottle of poteen from the cupboard.

'I'll be needing one of these, so,' he said, sitting at the table. 'Nancy?'

'Not home, yet.'

Brendan paused and knocked back a glass of poteen.

'And that's why you're worried?'

'Can you blame me?'

'No, son, I cannot. Listen, we'll sit for an hour and if she's not back, we'll take a walk and call on Brigid. Let there be no fear, she'll be fine, so.'

'Thanks. If you weren't here I think I'd lose my mind.'

'Best hang on to that, you've little else worth keeping.'

The front door slammed. Brendan raised a finger and pointed at his son.

'Hold your tongue,' he said quietly. 'Just be nice.'

Nancy paused as she entered the kitchen, aware that she'd interrupted an otherwise private conversation. She looked hungover, her eyes were puffy and swollen, her skin flushed by the cold and her hair, normally tamed by a band, cascaded around her shoulders in a rampant mess.

'Don't stop talking on my account,' she said, frowning at the pair of them as though they were uninvited guests. 'I'm only the housekeeper.'

Fearghus forced a smile.

'How was Brigid? Good craic?' he said.

Nancy said nothing, choosing instead to hijack Brendan's glass and the bottle of poteen.

'I was worried,' said Fearghus. 'We, were worried.'

Nancy stared blankly at the table.

'Worried? About me? And why would that be? Did you forget how use the stove?'

'Now, come on, Nancy, you know…'

'Have you no clean clothes? Is that it?'

Fearghus turned his attention to the can of beans.

'Nothing wrong with you then, is there?' he said, raising his voice.

'Meaning?'

'Where were you last night?'

'You know full well where I was,' said Nancy. 'Why the sudden concern?'

'Have you not heard?'

'You'll have to be more specific, Fearghus, my telepathy isn't great after a drink.'

Fearghus turned, leaned on the table and scowled at his wife.

'There was a fella found dead last night. Murdered, so he was.'

'You're joking me?' said Nancy. 'Murdered? Where?'

'At the hotel. The poor fella was hacked to pieces, carved open like a...'

'Sounds like he had a better night than me.'

'There's a feckin' madman on the loose and all you can do is joke about it?'

'Don't you go worrying, now, Fearghus, I can look after meself.'

'Aye, if there's one person you can look after, 'tis yourself, Nancy McBride, but I'll take no chances. Here. I want you to carry this, just in case.'

Fearghus tossed a farmer's blade on the table. Nancy, her eyes glazed with nostalgia, picked it up and gently stroked the weathered, rosewood handle. She carefully ran a finger along the edge of the 4" steel, scratched and scarred from years of use.

'Can hardly see the engraving, now,' she said, quietly. 'Happier times, eh, Fearghus?' She pushed it back across the table.

'I'll not need it,' she said. 'Start with a knife, next thing you know, it's a gun. You'll have me carrying the feckin' Purdey just to fetch the groceries, next.'

'Take it,' said Fearghus. 'I'll not hear otherwise.'

Nancy drained her glass, slipped the knife into her pocket and slowly raised her eyes to Fearghus.

'Sorry,' she whispered. 'Didn't meant to... I'm just tired, is all. I have a lot to think about, you know, what with the...'

'I know,' said Fearghus. 'I know. Don't you go worrying yourself. Don't worry about anything, now.'

She smiled and hauled herself from the chair.

'I need to wash, feel filthy, so I do. Be down after a bath.'

Muffled voices, barely audible, drifted up from the kitchen as Nancy rummaged through the foot of the wardrobe. Nestling towards the back, hidden beneath a heap of abandoned shoes and discarded scarves, she found the box. A plain, white box with a snug-fitting lid. Inside, wrapped in tissue with a handful of cards and a dried rose corsage, was her wedding dress, a simple, ivory affair bought by Brendan as a gift for a penniless bride. She smiled, fleetingly, as she recalled the day he walked her up the aisle, as proud as any father might have been, as proud as her own father might have been, perhaps, had he been there. Had she known who he was.

She pulled the wallet from her coat pocket and counted out the cash. Five hundred and fifty. She studied the driver's licence. If Josh Balducci was an average anything, his pin number would be hidden within his date of birth. She memorised it, stuffed the credit cards into her jacket pocket, pushed the wallet into the folds of the dress and returned the box to its resting place.

CHAPTER 4

Jack Molloy, unlike his over-enthusiastic sergeant, did not like surprises. Nor did he thrive on the unexpected. He was a creature of habit, enjoyed his routine and preferred to leave his desk at a reasonable hour. He wasn't particularly sociable and he wasn't keen on entertaining visitors either, especially those who pitched up unannounced and deprived him of his supper and a good night's sleep. Josh Balducci had managed to do both.

Having spent most of the night confined to a hotel room crammed with Scene of Crime Officers and a pathologist with a keen eye for detail, Molloy was glad to return to the relative calm of his somewhat antiquated office. Tired, he sat back and cradled a mug of tea as D.S. Hanagan, clearly unaffected by the lack of rest, stuck photos of the crime scene to the wall. Molloy hung his head in despair as, one by one, they slipped and glided gently to the floor.

'Can we not get one of those fancy boards, you know, like they have on the television?' he sighed.

Hanagan laughed.

'Dream on, Jack, this is the real world. TV budgets are bigger than ours.'

'Get some feckin' gaffer tape, then. It's bad enough not sleeping, I can't concentrate if they keep flying off the wall, too.'

Hanagan rummaged through his drawer for a box of drawing pins.

'I've been waiting for a case like this,' he said. 'Something I can get me teeth into. Do you not prefer a good murder, Jack? Something a wee bit taxing?'

Molloy drained his cup.

'Indeed I do, Sergeant. As long as it's on the feckin' TV and doesn't last more than an hour. Right, so, come on and let's have a run through before the fellas on Anglesea Street get wind of this and take it off our hands.'

'What?' said Hanagan, surprised at the notion. 'But this our case, the lads at HQ can't come down here and just take over... can they?'

'They can do what the feck they like, we're nothing but a bunch of culchies as far as they're concerned. Let's get cracking, first things first, from the top, it was one of his pals who found him, right?'

'That's right,' said Hanagan. 'There were four in the group. According to this fella, Carl Miller, they all had dinner at Finns Table then moved on to The Grey Hound, but Balducci went back to the hotel at the last minute, said he forgot his phone.'

'Have we checked it?' said Molloy.

'Yes. Only prints on the phone are his and the last call he made was four days ago, voicemail.'

Molloy raised his hand.

'Now, why,' he said, 'would he want to go back for his phone when he hadn't used it in four days?'

'No idea,' said Hanagan, with a shrug of the shoulders. 'Maybe he was expecting a call?'

'Or maybe he wasn't going back for the phone after all.'

'I don't follow.'

'Maybe, he didn't go back to the hotel,' said Molloy. 'Maybe he went somewhere else. Go on.'

'Miller and the others left The Grey Hound around five past ten and went back to the hotel. It was Miller who went to check on Balducci, see if he was alright, and that's when he got the fright of his life.'

'I bet he did,' said Molloy. 'Mark my words, sleep will not come easy for that fella, not tonight, that's for sure. How about his family? Did we find a next of kin?'

'None,' said Hanagan. 'According to Miller, he was an only child, parents died a few years back, so, no family at all.'

'No-one around to wave him off? Shame, I'd hate that, I would, being the last one to leave the party. Knowing my luck, I'll be in the same boat, be digging me own grave, so I will. Still, least I won't have to worry about paying for a wake. Anyway, what about the knife, did we get anything off that?'

'Nothing but a smudge. Apparently, it's the way the knife was held, there's a hint of a print, but nothing identifiable.'

'The way the knife was held? I wonder if that was deliberate, then?' said Molloy.

'How so?'

'Well, like he knew what he was doing, when he held the knife.'

'Maybe,' said Hanagan, 'I mean, he wasn't wearing gloves, so...'

'He wasn't wearing gloves, which makes me think he wasn't worried about getting caught. Which also makes me think he acted impulsively. Whoever did this, didn't go prepared, they didn't go with the intention of slaying the fella.'

'You think so?'

'I know so. If there was, the phrase they use in the films is, "malice aforethought", he'd have cleaned up after himself. He wouldn't have left the knife sticking in his back and he most certainly wouldn't have left those cups lying around, speaking of which?'

'Couldn't be better if we'd dabbed them ourselves,' said Hanagan. 'Perfect set of prints on both cups. We've got Balducci on one, but no match for the prints on the other, so I'd say whoever it was, hasn't been in trouble before.'

'You've a lot to learn, Sergeant,' said Molloy shaking his head. 'It just means they've never been caught.'

Hanagan paused and smirked.

'Right so, but now, here's an interesting thing, Jack. These other prints, the ones we can't identify, they're small, so, like a woman's…'

'Makes sense, so, single fella on his holidays…'

'But the skin on the fingers is tough and worn, calloused almost, like the hands of a, I don't know, a labourer.'

'So, a small fella, maybe?' said Molloy.

'Well, a fella with small hands, or a hard working lass.'

'A lass? No, I don't buy it, it doesn't fit. She'd have had to have been twenty stone and six feet tall to grapple with a fella that size. No, I reckon if there was a lass, she'd have left before the killer arrived. Anyway, the cups, they had whiskey in them, did we find the bottle?'

'No, not even an empty in the bin,' said Hanagan. 'The bartender remembers selling Balducci a bottle of Paddy's, though. He paid cash, the sale registered at 7.42pm but there's no sign of it.'

'I wish we knew where it was, could use a drop meself, right now. Okay, what else, I mean, like hairs, fibres, that kind of thing?'

'Nothing unusual. There were half a dozen hairs on the bed, maybe more, all different. Could've come from anywhere, previous occupant, his coat, the pub, the maid service. Even someone he might have, er, entertained.'

Molloy ran his fingers through his thinning crop of brown hair and sighed in frustration.

'This is going nowhere fast,' he said. 'We've a murder weapon and fingerprints, this should be feckin' easy. Do they not have any cameras about the place? The hotel? Like the old CCTV?'

'Only in the bar, and they're trained on the till,' said Hanagan.

'Great. And the street outside, don't suppose there's a camera there, is there?'

Hanagan raised his eyebrows and shook his head as Molloy, hands in pockets, paced the floor, irritated by the lack of progress.

'And no-one remembers seeing anyone else, coming or going,' he said. 'The staff, other guests, people in the restaurant?'

Hanagan grimaced apologetically as he delivered another negative answer.

'It's a bar and a hotel and a restaurant, Jack,' he said. 'Impossible to say who should've been there, and who shouldn't. I suppose whoever it was must have had one of those forgettable, faces.'

'Sounds like Mrs. Molloy. Holy shite, I should give her a call, she'll be worrying, so.'

'No need,' said Hanagan. 'She rang earlier, I told her you were tied up.'

Molloy sighed.

'Don't go giving her ideas,' he said. 'She's demanding enough as it is. Okay, what about I.D.?'

'Well, we have his passport, but that's it.'

'That's it? No wallet?' exclaimed Molloy.

'No wallet.'

'He's on holiday and he's no wallet? He's been robbed, so.'

'He might have lost it,' said Hanagan.

Molloy paused and bit his lip as he pondered the suggestion before dismissing it.

'No,' he said, confidently. 'He had it when he bought the whiskey, he paid cash, remember? Besides, if he'd lost

43

it, his pals would've known, they'd have helped him out. No, he didn't lose it. Someone took it. The fella that killed him took it, of that, I'm sure.'

Hanagan said nothing but waited patiently as Molloy clasped his hands behind his back and scrutinised the photos in the hope of spotting something they might have missed. He noticed a travel clock in one shot, on the floor, by the bedside table.

'Time of death,' he mumbled, as if thinking aloud. 'Time of death.'

'What's that?' said Hanagan.

'Time of death. He bought the whiskey at a quarter to eight, right? Miller found him at 10.20, and according to the pathologist, he'd only been dead a couple of hours.'

'What are you getting at?'

'Look here. See that?' said Molloy, 'The clock, on the floor, there. What time does it say?'

'About 8.10 by the looks of it.'

'8.10. The feckin' clock stopped when it hit the floor, at 8.10. That's when this fella was killed, give or take a couple of seconds.'

'Genius.'

'I know. So, whoever killed him must've been in the room when he went to buy the whiskey.'

'Unless he arranged to meet someone there,' said Hanagan.

'No, the window of opportunity is too small. If he'd arranged to meet someone there, they'd have had to have been as punctual as Big feckin' Ben. No, they were there already, and I reckon it was someone he knew.'

'Someone he knew? But all his pals were in the pub,' said Hanagan.

'You're telling me he's on holiday and he took a vow of silence? Spoke to no-one?'

'Well, no, I mean, I suppose it's possible.'

'It's definitely possible, he's American, and if there's one thing Americans like doing, it's talking, mainly about themselves. This fella, Miller, he says they were here for the golf, could've been someone he met there, did we check the club?'

'Yes, and before you ask, no, nothing. Not a sausage.'

Molloy turned on his heels and stabbed the air with his fist.

'That's it!' he said excitedly. 'Sausages! And mashed potato. Tap Tavern, lunch, I could eat a feckin' horse. We'll go as soon as the pathologist's been. He'll be here soon, meantime, get on to the embassy, we can't sit on a foreign national too long, someone'll kick up a stink. Oh, and ask them for a trace on his bank account, that kind of thing. Someone took his wallet so you never know, we might get lucky.'

* * *

At 6'1" and weighing barely more than ten stone, Tom McKinley was used to attracting glances, usually from small children who clung to their mother's skirts out of sheer terror. He looked older than his years and the shock of thick, white hair atop his grey, gaunt face suggested he'd witnessed something traumatic in the past. He paused outside the Garda station on Church Square, extinguished his cigarette, and went inside.

'If it isn't the butcher of Ballyglasheen,' said Molloy, grinning. 'Thanks for coming, Tom, will you take a coffee?'

'I will,' said the softly spoken McKinley. 'It's been a long night.'

'You should've gone home, no need to kill yourself.'

''Tisn't a problem. I prefer working at night.'

'I bet you do,' said Molloy, passing him a mug.

'Although, if truth be known,' said McKinley, 'there's a lot to be said for two-way conversations. In my line of work, they tend to be a little one-sided, if you get what I mean.'

Molloy smiled and offered the pathologist his chair.

'I do that,' he said. 'With me, it's Mrs. Molloy, she does all the talking, I can't get a word in edgeways. So, Hanagan here, he's all ears, what have you got for us?'

McKinley leaned back, clasped his hands beneath his chin and stared at Hanagan with his steely, blue eyes.

'Are you fond of the bodies, Sergeant?' he said, quietly. 'Those that have, expired, I mean?'

Hanagan almost choked on his coffee.

'Well, no, I mean, can't say I... although, there is something...'

'Fascinating,' said McKinley. 'There is something... fascinating about the human body, especially when you realise how frail and vulnerable it really is.'

'Right, so. I'm not sure I'd...'

'How's your stomach, Sergeant? Do you have a strong constitution?'

'I suppose, I mean, I'm not prone to throwing...'

'Then you must come and watch some time. You might learn something. Anyway, to the case in hand, how far have you got?' asked McKinley.

Molloy sighed.

'Not far, Tom,' he said. 'I was hoping you might give us something to go on.'

'Right you are. Well, first of all, I have to say it was very considerate of the fella to leave us the knife. You've no idea how frustrating it can be, sometimes, trying to figure out what someone used to hack a fella to shreds.'

'I've a theory, so,' said Hanagan, leaping from his desk. 'Balducci, see, he turns his back on the assailant, like this, and as he does so, the killer takes the opportunity to strike, stabs him in the back and slices him open. Naturally, being dead and all, he falls flat on the bed.'

Molloy cocked his head, accepting the theory as plausible, until McKinley intervened.

'Very good, Sergeant, not bad at all,' he said, walking towards Hanagan. 'But completely wrong. Here, I'd like to show you something, bear with me a moment. Now, you would say, would you not, that I am about the same height as the victim?'

'You are, so,' said Hanagan, smiling enthusiastically.

'And *you*, for the sake of argument, are about average height?'

'I am that.'

McKinley turned his back on Hanagan and stood stock still.

'Now, pretend you have the knife,' he said. 'I want you to stab me in the back, take care, mind, to stab me where you think the blade first entered the body.'

Hanagan, grinning wildly, as though he were taking part in a stage show, glanced at Molloy and stabbed McKinley in the small of his back with his index finger.

'Excellent,' said the pathologist, 'excellent. Now, I want you to slice me open.'

Molloy laughed aloud as he watched Hanagan raise his arm and stop less than midway along McKinley's back, unable to lift it any farther.

'Feckin' genius, Tom!' he said. 'So, how'd he do it? What really happened?'

McKinley turned to face Hanagan.

'I'll show you,' he said. 'Like this. Now, you were right about the point of entry, Sergeant, full marks for that, but the killer wasn't behind the victim, he was facing him.'

'Facing him?' said Molloy.

'Staring him in the eyes, so he was.'

McKinley placed one hand on Hanagan's shoulder and demonstrated with the other behind his back.

'The blade entered the back here, and was dragged, forcefully, the length of the spine. Judging by the angle and the depth of the cut, it's also obvious the killer was right handed. The blade was removed when it got here, towards the top of the shoulder blades, I'd say that's when your man all but expired. Just for good measure, he was then stabbed in the neck here, severing the spinal cord. That finished him off.'

'Pardon the old French, Tom,' said Molloy, 'but feckin' hell, he must have been a big fella then, are we looking for someone as tall yourself?'

McKinley returned to his chair.

'No, Jack. There's something else the angle and the depth of the blade can tell us. The fella you're looking for needn't be that big, average height, maybe even smaller, but here's the thing. They weren't standing up, they were lying down. He was beneath the victim.'

'What?' exclaimed Molloy.

'The victim was lying on top of his killer.'

'Are you sure?'

'Is the Pope Italian?'

'No.'

'I'm still sure,' said McKinley.

'What the hell would he be doing on top of another fella?' said Molloy.

Hanagan, almost embarrassed, proffered a suggestion.

'You don't think he was, you know, I mean…'

'It's possible,' said McKinley. 'I'd say he and his assailant were in the throes of something passionate when he was killed. There were traces of semen on his shorts.'

'And you're sure it wasn't a lass?' asked Molloy.

'Well, it's possible, but I can't see it meself,' said McKinley, 'unless she was incredibly strong. She'd have to be a dab hand with a knife, too.'

Molloy let out an exasperated sigh.

'Ah, well, still none the wiser, then,' he said. 'Thanks for coming, Tom. You've been a great help, so.'

McKinley stood and took a cigarette from his pocket in preparation for the walk back to his car.

''Tis a pleasure, Jack. Anything else I can help you with?'

'Not unless you can come up with a motive,' said Molloy.

McKinley, somewhat amused by the question, cracked a smile and laughed aloud.

'A motive?' he asked. 'Well, I doubt it would be the usual, Jack, you know, robbery or the like. Could be revenge, maybe. Or jealousy. Or, it may simply be the result of someone's perverse sense of... pleasure.'

'Don't stop there,' said Molloy, intrigued by his response. 'Tell us more.'

McKinley took the cigarette from his mouth and sat back down.

'Well, it's only my opinion, but apart from the few items on the floor, there was no real sign of a struggle, so it could've been the result of an argument, perhaps. It may have been impulsive.'

Molloy rubbed his hands.

'I'm right so far, then.'

'However,' said McKinley, 'I'd say 'twas more likely your man knew his assailant and was lured into that position.'

'Lured?'

'Indeed. They were getting intimate, shall we say. I'd say whoever did this enticed your victim with the promise of one thing, and delivered something else.'

'Why?' asked Hanagan.

'That's your department, Sergeant,' said McKinley, 'but my guess is this Balducci fella just happened to pick up the wrong man, or girl.'

'So,' said Molloy, hesitating as he digested Tom's analysis, 'you're saying whoever did this wasn't your regular "opportunist", they kind of planned it, but they weren't bothered about who they got?'

'Correct. Oh, and I don't think they're too concerned about getting caught either. Dare say they get a wee buzz from leaving a few clues behind, to torment you, like.'

'Do you... do you think they'll do it again?' Molloy whispered, fearful of the answer.

'There's a good chance, so. If I'm right, people with this kind of, let's call it a desire, rarely stop at the one. It's like the old nicotine, once you start, 'tis a terrible job trying to give up.'

Molloy reached for his coat.

'So,' he said, 'we're looking for a fella of average height with a strong right arm who may or may not be gay, or, a big lass who knows how to use a knife and is fond of the old whiskey. Sure, 'tis a piece of cake, we'll have this wrapped up by teatime. I have to eat before I fall over, will you join us for lunch, Tom?'

'Thanks, no, they've a special in the canteen today. Liver and tripe.'

CHAPTER 5

Try as he might, Fearghus could not relax. He was used to
working twelve hours a day, sometimes more, but with no
sheep to tend to and the top field already ploughed in
preparation for the barley, the days were starting to drag.
The trip to Clouracaun, much to his annoyance, did not
take as long as he expected. Having dropped off the
concentrates for the sheep, he returned home at a leisurely
pace, thankful, at least, that they now had enough cash for
a sow and six weaners. It wasn't much, but it would be a
start.

Considering the time, fast approaching 11am, the house
was unusually quiet. Brendan, according to the note left on
the kitchen table, was out digging for gold and would not
return until the afternoon. Fearghus swore. Nancy, as
usual, was nowhere to be seen. Concerned though he was
about her malaise, he was even more frustrated by her
complete lack of interest in anything concerning the farm.
He made a call and arranged to meet the pig breeder later
that day. All being well, he would take delivery of the herd
by the end of the week.

'Ah, 'tis the sleeping beauty,' he said, as Nancy sauntered into the kitchen.

She scowled at his sarcasm, helped herself to a glass of milk and knocked back a pill.

'Headache?' he asked.

'Not really,' she said. 'No.'

Fearghus, desperate to cheer her up, slammed the table with the palm of his hand.

'Well, I've good news!' he crowed. 'We'll be back in business by the end of the week. Best hose down the old wellies, you'll be needing them, so!'

'What do you mean?' said Nancy, folding her arms. 'What exactly do you mean?'

'The Landrace. I've just called the fella, in Skibbereen. I'm going to see him now. By the end of the week we'll have our litter, plus, wait for it, he'll let us have the loan of a boar when the sow's on heat, so we'll breeding in no time, isn't that great?'

Nancy was either unimpressed or uninterested, it was difficult to ascertain which.

'And we'll pay for them, how?' she said.

'With the money from the concentrates. I have it here.'

'And you've thought this through?'

'I have indeed.'

'You're sure, now? Because, Fearghus, I see no sign of a pen out there, no fencing and no ark.'

'Sure, 'tis just a case of driving a few poles in the ground, it'll only take a couple of days.'

'How will we feed them? How will we pay for that?'

'Don't you go worrying yourself, it'll cost next to nothing. They'll be on pasture most of the year. Trust me, Nancy, I know what I'm doing, I'm on the case.'

'So am I. I'm away to fetch some groceries. I'll not be eating beans on toast again.'

'Hold on, don't you want to talk about this? I mean, first you tear me head off because we've no plan for the future, and now that we do, you still can't be bothered. It's like you want us to fail, like you want us to give up.'

'I'm ahead of you, there, Fearghus,' she said. 'I'm ahead of you, there.'

* * *

Pearse Street was the usual lunchtime throng of office workers and clueless tourists dressed in mountaineering jackets searching for something other than crubeens and colcannon to eat. Nancy, head down, walked briskly past the Blue Haven and cursed the queue of people waiting to use the cash machine outside the Allied Irish Bank. She paused for a moment as she struggled to recall the location of the other banks in the town, then scurried down to Emmet Place. There was hardly a soul to be seen, the Bank of Ireland was empty and no-one was using the ATM. She glanced cautiously up and down the street before retrieving one of Balducci's cards from her pocket. Chase Bank, Visa. She slipped it into the machine. Her heart pounded as she tentatively keyed in a number.

1980.

'Invalid PIN'.

'Shite.'

1122.

'Invalid PIN'.

'For feck's sake.'

8019.

'CARD BLOCKED'.

'Dammit!' she muttered, as it spat back the card.

Her hands, clammy and cold, trembled with a mix of fear and excitement as she pulled a second card from her pocket and rehearsed a number in her head. The ATM silently sucked the Citibank Platinum into its bowels and requested a PIN. Nancy took a deep breath and slowly tapped the keypad.

2280.

'Come on, come on,' she hissed, as the machine made up its mind.

'SELECT SERVICE'.

'Yes!' She glanced over her shoulder and stabbed the 'CASH' button.

'ENTER AMOUNT'.

'500'.

The ATM fell silent as it considered her request, almost as though it knew what she was doing. It made her wait, and wait, and wait, before suddenly whirring into action and dispensing a fistful of fifties. She stuffed the cash into her pocket, turned her collar up against the cold and any passers-by, and headed towards the main street.

The Armada was as dark as a coal cellar and, in the absence of drinkers, just as inviting. A shot of whiskey steadied her nerves. The second made her anxious to return home. The lunchtime crowds had disappeared. Pearse Street was relatively quiet and the cash machine outside the Allied Irish Bank was devoid of customers. The temptation was too great. She bolted across the street, shoved the Chase card into the slot and, in an effort to unlock it, typed in the same number. The ATM was generous to a fault and didn't hesitate in complying with her request for 1,000.

Fearghus flinched as the front door slammed. He sighed and prepared himself for another barrage of abuse as Brendan, buried in the local paper, wisely kept his head down.

'You're both here!' said Nancy, as she barged into the kitchen. 'Grand! I hope you're hungry!'

She dropped the bags on the floor, threw her arms around her husband's neck and kissed him on the cheek.

'Jesus, was that a happy pill you took this morning?' he said.

'You might say that,' she said. 'So, did you sort things out in Skibereen?'

'I did, that. What have you been up to?'

'Shopping. Now, what will we have? I've chops, steaks, a chicken or a roast.'

Brendan looked up from his paper.

'Am I in the right house?' he asked.

Nancy walked around the table and pecked the top of his head.

'You are so.'

Fearghus eyed the groceries.

'Nancy,' he asked, hesitating for fear of ruining the atmosphere, 'how did you... I mean, all this, it must've cost a bit...'

Nancy smiled.

'Don't you go worrying yourself, now. I've been putting some aside every week, so we could have a holiday, like, but that'll have to wait. Food is more important.'

'I could kiss you,' said Fearghus.

'What's stopping you? Come, so.'

Brendan watched and smiled as they embraced.

'It's good to have you back,' he said.

Nancy smiled and turned to Fearghus.

'I've something else for you,' she said, handing him a bundle of notes. 'Here, you'll need this, for the fencing and the ark, and if there's any left over, maybe you could buy yourself some more pork.'

Fearghus was lost for words.

'But, but, there's a feckin' fortune here, how did...'

'It's the rest of the holiday money. No point in sitting on it.'

Fearghus stared at the wad of cash and shook his head.

'I love you, Nancy McBride,' he sighed.

Nancy winked, emptied the bags and tossed three striploins into a pan as Fearghus opened a bottle of wine and sat by his father.

'Anything interesting, Da?' he asked, filling the glasses.

'Same old shite,' said Brendan. 'Will you see here, the car park down by the quay, they're closing it to build more fancy apartments, as if we don't have enough already.'

'That's progress for you,' said Fearghus. 'Is there no good news? Nothing about a kitten being rescued from a tree, maybe?'

'No, just that eejit, McCabe. Needs rescuing from himself, so he does. He just got out of prison for using a stolen credit card and does the same thing, again. Did he not get himself an education? You'd have thought he'd have had the sense to go somewhere else and do it, somewhere he's not known, not where he feckin' lives.'

Nancy froze.

'I'll take a glass of that,' she said, pointing towards the wine, 'unless you're planning on drinking it all yourself.' She knocked it back. 'I was thinking, you'll be busy tomorrow, what with the pen and all, so I might have meself a day out, clear me head and get used to the pig thing before I get stuck in.'

Fearghus raised his glass.

'That's a grand idea,' he said, 'you deserve it. Where will you go?'

'Not sure, Waterford, maybe.'

'Waterford? That means the bus, time it takes you could be in Dublin on the train.'

'Right, so. I'll think about it.'

CHAPTER 6

Nancy stepped from the bus and stretched her legs. Two hours staring at nothing but green fields and trees, with a driver who'd swallowed the Blarney Stone, was enough to make her yearn for a life in the city surrounded by concrete and pigeons. She crossed the tarmac, away from the stench of diesel, and gazed vacantly across the River Suir. It was as still as a mill pond, with not even a row boat to ripple its surface. The view opposite, yet more trees and a busy road, soon became tiresome. She checked her pocket for Balducci's legacy and left.

Unlike the bustling city centre, there was no frenzy of activity in the cafés and bars along The Quay, no office workers malingering over coffee, fearful of returning to their desks, just the occasional car nipping by and the sound of gulls hovering overhead. A fifteen minute stroll took her to Barronstrand Street where, on the opposite corner, much to her surprise, stood a deserted branch of the AIB. She smiled, walked casually towards the ATM, and pulled the last of Balducci's unused cards from her pocket. She gave it a cursory glance, 'Hudson City Savings Bank', and pushed it gently into the slot. Hoping he'd led a life uncomplicated by PINs and passwords, she slowly and deliberately tapped out the same number as before.

'Come on,' she moaned, impatient at the machine's lethargic approach to verifying the number. 'Come on, you feckin'... come on, come on.'

Her cheeks puffed with relief as the screen flashed and offered up the usual menu. She was about to hit 'CASH', when, at the very last moment, her eyes settled on another option. She took a deep breath and stabbed the button next to 'VIEW BALANCE'.

'Sweet feckin' Jesus,' she breathed as '$23,011.48' flashed onto the screen.

With nothing to lose, she chanced her arm and requested a withdrawal of 1,000. The machine clicked and whirred with the strain of counting out the notes until finally, exhausted, it spat out the cash. Having pillaged Balducci's account, she wandered back along The Quay, checked her watch and cursed. It was too early to board the bus home. If her journey to Waterford as a self-indulgent day-trip was to be believed, she would have to linger for at least a couple of hours. MC's Outdoor Store proved a timely distraction. Judging by the lack of customers, it was obviously not, she thought, the camping season. She wandered silently amongst the tents and the camping stoves, the hiking boots and the waterproofs, the rucksacks and the sleeping bags, when the inevitable occurred. A sales assistant scuttled across the floor like a grinning beetle and abused her ears with a barrage of meaningless banter before plucking up the courage to pop the inevitable question.

'So, what can we help you with today, madam?' he asked. Nancy glared at the man and frowned.

'We?' she said, looking around.

'Alright, I mean, me.'

She winced as she struggled to find an excuse to leave when, in a flash of inspiration, she said, 'I'm looking for a present. A couple of gifts. For me husband and the father-in-law.'

'Anything in particular?'

'Something easy to carry, so I'll not be wanting a feckin' frame tent.'

The assistant smiled.

'Would you maybe give me a clue, or will I try to guess, like that game, charades, I think they call it.'

Nancy thought of Brendan, digging in the silt and the mud for a handful of worthless, rusty, old coins.

'Gloves,' she said. 'Good, strong, waterproof gloves.'

'Size?'

She held up her hand. 'Bigger than this.'

The assistant picked out a pair of tough, leather gloves with a thermal inner and held them up for approval like a grovelling sommelier in an over-priced restaurant.

'I'm guessing they'll not be the cheapest ones you have,' she said.

The assistant blushed.

'I can get you something else, we have some cheaper ones over…'

'Don't trouble yourself,' she said as she eyed the display cabinet by the counter.

The assistant followed discreetly and peered over her shoulder.

'That's a great model, that,' he said, pointing at the top shelf.

'What is?'

'That compass, there, you'll have no trouble finding north with a piece like that.'

Nancy turned to the assistant and glowered.

'Do I look like Marco feckin' Polo?' she said. 'We're farmers, not explorers. I'll take that knife, there, the Leatherman.'

The salesman gleefully retrieved it from the cabinet, delighted by the fact that it was substantially more expensive than a plastic, Taiwanese compass. He fleetingly entertained the notion of a night in the pub followed by a kebab until Nancy handed him a bank card rather than cash. His face dropped as he reluctantly accepted it and apologised for the lack of gift wrap.

'Hudson City?' he said. 'Looks fancy, I've not seen one of these before.'

'It's me bank, where we live,' said Nancy.

'I thought you were Irish?'

'I am feckin' Irish, doesn't mean I have to live here. We live in New York, Larchmont, it's a village, bit like Kinsale, on the water, so it is.'

'Sounds grand. Oh, one last thing, would you have any I.D?'

'I.D?' said Nancy, puzzled.

'You have to be over twenty-one to buy the knife,' said the salesman.

Nancy dropped her head in embarrassment and regarded him with her big, doe eyes.

'Are you single?' she asked.

A smile of anticipation crept across his face. 'I am that,' he said, smugly.

'I'm not surprised.'

Nancy retraced her steps and, ambling past the AIB, allowed herself a smug smile, as if recalling an illicit night of passion. Balducci's plastic was burning a hole in her pocket. She retained the card from the Hudson City Savings Bank, wrapped the others in the bag from the outdoor store and surreptitiously dropped it into a waste bin.

The Gingerman was everything a visitor in search of old Irish charm could want from a pub: floor to ceiling timber panelling, sandblasted mirrors, platefuls of bacon and cabbage and The Dubliners blaring from the stereo. Nancy sat with a half a pint of Murphy's and a whiskey chaser and gazed out across the tiny cobbled street, her mind a blank. An hour, she thought, then she'd head for home and cite boredom as the reason for her premature return.

'Would you mind?'

An affable-looking gent in his late fifties with a warm smile and a face etched with history was clutching a large glass of red. His hair matched his suit, neat and grey.

'I'm sorry?' she said, annoyed at the interruption.

'Would you mind, if I sat here? Would I be intruding?' he asked softly.

Nancy glanced around the pub and sighed.

'I don't believe it,' she whined. 'There's a bar full of empty chairs and you have to sit here?'

He stood his ground and smiled.

'Ah, well,' she said, reluctantly, 'suit yourself, but I'm telling you now, I'll not talk to strangers.'

'We're not strangers,' he said, 'just friends that haven't met.'

Nancy rolled her eyes.

The man said nothing, sat opposite, clasped his hands beneath his chin and joined her in staring out of the window. The silence was as uncomfortable as a dinner date with someone she despised.

'Come on then,' she said in defeat. 'The suspense is killing me. Let's have it.'

'Have what?' he said.

'The life story. The cheating wife, the bad business deal, whatever, just make it quick.'

The man cocked his head inquisitively.

'You've a terrible anger for a young lass,' he said. 'I can leave if you like.'

'Reverse psychology? Make me feel guilty so I plead with you to stay?'

'It often works.'

Nancy sipped the porter and wiped her lips with the back of her hand.

'Sorry,' she said, 'didn't mean to be rude. Go on then, where you from?'

The old man took a mouthful of wine and grimaced.

'Connecticut,' he said.

'Connecticut? You don't sound like a Yank.'

'I'm not. I was born in Sligo. Eamon's the name. Eamon Reilly.'

'Good for you.'

'I was dragged across the water at the tender age of fifteen. Me father thought we'd be happy there. He was wrong. Forty-four years I've been there and forty-four years I've hated it.'

'Why don't you leave?'

'Ah, now, there's a question, and I wish I had the answer. Truth is, I don't know. I just got kind of, settled, I suppose.'

Nancy regarded him suspiciously.

'Then, why are you here now?' she asked. 'You don't look like the kind of fella that gets homesick.'

'I don't. Not for Sligo, anyway. I'm here on business.'

'Business. Let me guess, you've come to buy a hotel, or, or...'

'Actually, I have a very boring job with a very large department store. As a buyer. Homeware, would you believe.'

'I'm so bored I'd believe anything, right now. Enlighten me, what exactly are you buying?'

'Glassware, of course, why else would I be in Waterford?'

'Well, if it's so boring, why don't you change jobs?'

'Complacency,' said Eamon, 'and a ridiculous salary. They think because I'm Irish I can do no wrong.'

'Must be the accent.'

'It's the one thing I've held on to. I always thought that if I lost that, I'd lose everything I believe in.'

'And what do you believe in?' asked Nancy.

'Oh, not much. Fate, I suppose. And people. Human nature. Unfortunately, 'tis a belief riddled with disappointment.'

'Disappointment?'

Eamon scratched the back of his head as he attempted to explain his philosophy.

'Well, we're all different see, you, me, that fella behind the bar, there, that's what makes life so interesting. But Americans… Americans can be so… so uniformly demanding, so, opinionated. No humility.'

Nancy grinned and knocked back the whiskey.

'You're not wrong there,' she said. 'Shameless, so they are.'

'You don't like Americans?'

'I have my reasons.'

Eamon returned the smile and pushed his glass to one side.

'I wouldn't insult a plate of chips with that stuff,' he said. 'Would you do me the honour…'

'Nancy.'

'Would you do me the honour, Nancy, of allowing me to buy you a drink?'

Eamon was not quite old enough to be her father and probably not young enough to be a lover, but judging by the twinkle in his eye, there was no doubt in her mind that he was quite the charmer.

'I will that,' she said, warming to his roguish allure. 'Murphy's.'

The pub slowly filled with whinging workers as Nancy listened, enthralled by the self-deprecating raconteur who joked about his childhood by the sea, working his way through college and living in a state where it's illegal to walk backwards after sunset, educate dogs, kiss your wife on a Sunday and exceed 65mph on a bicycle.

'So,' he said, 'you can see why I get frustrated with me neighbours. How about you?'

'Me?'

'What turned you against our transatlantic cousins?'

'It's a long story.'

Eamon sat back and folded his arms.

'There's nowhere I have to be,' he said with a smirk.

Nancy hesitated, took a slug of whiskey and looked him in the eye.

'Are you sure you work for a department store?' she said jokingly. 'You sound like a feckin' therapist, or a peeler, even.'

'Would it bother you if I was?' asked Eamon.

His response unsettled her. She hesitated and toyed nervously with a tress of hair.

'No. Why would it? I've nothing to hide.'

'Well, then. Of course, if you'd rather not, I'd quite understand.'

Her shoulders slumped with relief. There was something about Eamon Reilly, be it his placid demeanour or the way he seemed to hang on her every word, that commanded trust and compelled her to share a morsel of her past that not even her husband knew about.

'Okay,' she said, surprised at how comfortable she felt in his company. 'A long time ago, me mother, see, had a fling, a one night stand, with this fella.'

'Glad to hear it was a fella.'

'He was a soldier, stationed in Belfast.'

'That'll be an American soldier, then?'

'Right so. He was down on leave, just the weekend, like. Anyway, after he'd, you know, had his fun, he left. Didn't even say goodbye. Me Mammy woke at three in the morning to find the wind howling through the house and the back door swinging on its hinges. He didn't even leave a note. Two weeks later he was back in Illinois, and nine months later, well, you can guess.'

Eamon shook his head.

'Terrible,' he said. 'I can only imagine how hard that must've been for your mother back then, having the baby out of wedlock, and all. Could she not... would she not have considered...'

'Are you joking me?' said Nancy. 'In this feckin' country? Come on, Eamon, you should know better than that.'

'Sorry, I wasn't thinking, it was a silly thing to say, I...'

'Doesn't matter. Anyway, the day after that baby celebrated her eighteenth birthday, me Mammy killed herself.'

'What?'

'True enough.'

'Dear God, I am sorry, Nancy. And this girl, she was your sister, then?'

Nancy smiled.

'I'm an only child, Eamon. I'm what you might call, a bastard.'

Eamon sat back, flabbergasted.

'Well,' he said, with a cheeky grin, 'if you don't mind me saying so, I think you're probably the loveliest bastard I've ever met.'

Nancy, cheeks flushing, squirmed with embarrassment at the unexpected compliment.

'And it seems I'm not the only one who thinks so.'

'What's that, now?'

'That fella behind you, standing at the bar like he's waiting for no-one, he's done nothing but stare ever since he walked in.'

'Let him look, I'm not interested.'

The temptation, and the curiosity, was too much to bear. Glancing around, as though searching for a wall clock or a sign for the ladies bathroom, she caught sight of a tall, lanky man with hair as black as jet and skin as white as the driven snow. Their eyes locked, momentarily, for less than a split of a second. She spun back in her seat and rummaged frantically through her jacket.

'Christ!' she muttered under her breath. 'Feckin' Jesus...'

She pulled a plastic strip of tablets from a pocket and popped the foil in search of a pill. It was empty.

'Jesus, feckin' Christ! I don't believe…'

'Are you okay?' asked Eamon, his brow furrowed with concern. 'Is it a headache you have? Can I…'

'No,' said Nancy, 'No, it's…yes, a headache, came on all of a sudden, I should…'

The skinny man appeared silently at the table, drink in hand.

'Cathleen? Sorry,' he said, glancing at Eamon, 'I don't mean to interrupt but, Cathleen, it is you, isn't it? Cathleen Moran?'

Nancy swilled the whiskey round the glass and spoke without looking up.

'I think you're mistaken. The name's Nancy, not that it's any of your business.'

'Ah, come so, Cathleen, I'd recognise you anywhere! It's me, Jim, Jim Dooley, from the hospital, St. Dympna's.'

'Saint what?' she said. 'I've never been to a hospital in me life, never heard of it.'

'Ah, sure you have, in Carlow, we were there…'

'I told you, me name's Nancy! Now, if you don't feck off, I'm going to…'

Eamon slowly rose to his feet and gently took the man by the elbow.

'Come on, son,' he said, 'you heard the young lady, be a good lad now and move on.'

'Ah, come now, Cathleen, why don't you just…'

'Listen,' said Eamon, 'if you persist in annoying me niece, I'll call the police meself.'

'Your niece?'

'That's what I said.'

'Oh. Sorry. My mistake then.' He glanced at the empty strip of pills lying on the table. 'Just odd, so it is, that you take the same pills as Cathleen, I mean, what are the chances of…'

'Away, now,' said Eamon. 'I'll not ask again.'

Jim Dooley shook his head and skulked back to the bar.

'Thanks,' said Nancy, 'for, you know... I should go now, it's getting late and I've a way to go.'

'So soon? And we were having such a wonderful time.'

'We were. Past tense.'

'Look, don't let that fella ruin your day. Mistaken identity, that's all it is. Come now, will you take another drink? One for the road, maybe?'

Nancy looked at Eamon and smiled lamely.

'I'd like that,' she said, 'but not here. I can't relax with that stalker peering over me shoulder.'

'We'll go somewhere quiet then. How about me hotel? It's just around the corner and it has a lovely bar, like an old gentlemen's club, so it is.'

'Grand,' said Nancy. 'I just need to freshen up and make a quick phone call.'

Eamon watched as Nancy went in search of the ladies, waited til she'd disappeared from view, then sidled up to the stalker at the bar.

'Dooley, you say your name was? Jim Dooley?' he asked.

'That's right, Sir.'

'I must apologise for me niece, she's not normally so snappy. Just a bit stressed, so. Work, you know how it is.'

'Ah, sure, no bother, it's just that, it's just... I could've sworn it was Cathleen. Sure, you've a double in her, there.'

'Tell me, if you don't me asking, who is this Cathleen? An ex-girlfriend?'

Jim smiled, as though he'd entertained the thought before.

'She was at St. Dympna's, that's where I used to work, as a nurse.'

'And she was a nurse, too?' asked Eamon.

'Oh, no. She was a patient.'

'A patient? Sure, she couldn't have been there long, you must have a good memory.'

'She was there four years and seven months,' said Dooley.

'What?' said Eamon, surprised at the duration of her stay. 'I've never heard of anyone staying in a hospital so long, they normally die within a couple of weeks.'

Jim laughed and downed what was left of his pint.

'Excuse me,' he said, 'you're obviously not familiar with St. Dympna's. It's a psychiatric hospital.'

'Is that so?'

'Indeed.'

'And what was this Cathleen doing there?' said Eamon.

'Cathleen Moran was found guilty of manslaughter. Killed a fella, so they say, American lad, up in Kilkenny. They sectioned her when they found out she was a manic depressive and a bit, unstable, like. She served the minimum, and then some. They released her, oh, must be about ten years ago, now. You wouldn't know it to look her, beautiful lass, so she was.'

'Thanks, Mr. Dooley,' said Eamon. 'Fascinating, so it is. Oh, one more thing, what was that you mentioned about the pills, sure, me niece has a headache is all.'

Jim tapped his nose with his forefinger and winked.

'Well, if I were you,' he said, 'I'd have a word with your niece, or her parents. Those aren't headache tablets, they're Tryptizol, anti-depressants. If you don't keep up the dosage…'

'I can assure you, Mr. Dooley, me niece is quite sound. She's no bats in the belfry.'

CHAPTER 7

Molloy closed the window against the deafening peal of the bells from St. Multose, perched on the window ledge and regarded his sergeant with an inquisitive smirk.

'What?' said Hanagan. 'Have you thought of a joke?'

'No, I was just thinking,' said Molloy, ruefully. 'Do you remember how it was when you joined the Garda? When you first arrived here?'

'I do that.'

'Carefree, no responsibility to speak of. Just pounding the streets, helping old ladies across the road, do you not miss that?'

'Miss it? You must be joking, God, it was boring, I mean...'

'Then get your feet off the feckin' desk and crack on or you'll be back on the beat before you know it.'

'Sir.'

'So, where have we got?'

'Well, let's see, uniform have interviewed Balducci's pals, again, all the staff at the hotel and some of the folk who were dining there. No-one's seen anything.'

'I just don't get it,' said Molloy as he returned to his desk. 'Way things are looking, he must've been killed by a feckin' poltergeist. Someone must've seen something, someone...'

'Maybe we should put out an appeal,' said Hanagan, 'for witnesses, on the television, like.'

Molloy slammed his fist on the table.

'That's a grand idea!' he exclaimed. 'We'll tell the whole country a madman's sliced a fella in two, he's on the loose and we've no idea who he is or what he looks like but don't worry, so, we'll find him soon enough. Don't be an arse.'

'Fair point.'

Molloy froze and stared at Hanagan wide-eyed.

'Madman,' he said quietly, rising to his feet and clicking his fingers.

'You've lost me,' said Hanagan.

'What if, what if this wasn't a one off? What if the killer is someone with a record, someone just a little bit, deranged?'

'You mean like Jack the Ripper or the Boston Strangler?' asked Hanagan.

'Right so, but with a much lower body count. Check the hospitals and the loony bins, I mean, the mental institutions, see if they've misplaced anyone recently. Anyone with a tendency to unzip people with a pocket knife.'

'Leave it to me.'

Hanagan scrambled to his feet, pulled on his coat and made for the door, notebook in hand.

'Hold on,' said Molloy, raising his hand. 'Something else. What if, what if this fella knew what he was doing?'

'You mean, like, he deliberately went after Balducci?'

'No, no,' said Molloy, 'We've been through that already. Do you not remember what Tom said, about the how the knife was dragged up the spine, severing the nerves?'

'I do.'

'Well, if you were in that situation, there's a big fella atop of you and you have a knife, would you not just stab him? In a frenzy? Stab, stab, stab, dead. Why slice them up the back and put them through that agony?'

'Obviously wasn't in a rush,' joked Hanagan.

'No. He wasn't,' said Molloy. 'He was calm. And he wanted to make him suffer. That's me point, he knew what he was doing. It's like he knew how to use a knife, like a butcher. He knew where to cut.'

'Right, so! Might not be a butcher though, could be a surgeon, I suppose, or, or someone who works in an abattoir, maybe?'

'Exactly. Come on, chop, chop. No time to lose.'

Hanagan turned for the door and paused.

'Oh, Jack, I almost forgot, there was one other thing,' he said.

Molloy, unimpressed, looked at him forlornly. 'And what would that be?' he sighed.

'We heard back from the embassy, got details on his bank account and his credit cards.'

'Well, that's something, I suppose. Mind you, I doubt we'll get anywhere with that, the poor fella's dead.'

'Actually…' said Hanagan, looking sheepishly towards the floor.

'What?' said Molloy. 'I'm going to regret asking this, I know I am, but what?'

'His credit cards. They were, erm, they were used. Yesterday.'

The church bells fell silent and a deathly hush descended on the office. Molloy closed his eyes and counted to three in the mistaken belief that he'd misheard what the sergeant had said.

'I beg your pardon?' he whispered.

'Balducci's credit cards,' said Hanagan. 'They were used at the ATM yesterday, down the road, so. Bank of Ireland, I think it was.'

'So this lunatic's still here in Kinsale and you didn't think to mention it?' bellowed Molloy. 'Are you a professional feckin' eejit? When did you find this out?'

'Erm, not long, couple of... last night. But it was late, I didn't want to, must've slipped me mind.'

'For feck's sake! Anything else?'

Hanagan cowered in anticipation of another verbal onslaught.

'Erm, I don't think he's in Kinsale anymore,' he said slowly.

'What?'

'This morning. Another one of his cards was used this morning, well, lunchtime, actually. In Waterford.'

'Jesus, Mary and Joseph! Do you like keeping secrets, Sergeant? Did you not call the bank and tell them to stop the cards? Have you...'

'I thought about it,' protested Hanagan. 'I thought about it, but...'

'But what?'

'I thought, I thought if the fella using the cards is the same fella that killed him, we might have a chance of finding him if, if we tracked him, when he takes out the cash, like.'

Molloy stared at his sergeant, took a deep breath and slowly cracked a smile.

'Have you given your brain a full time job? Sure, it's been on the minimum wage long enough,' he said. 'For once you've accomplished something approaching intelligent. Call the bank in Waterford, tell them we need the CCTV as soon as possible.'

'All done, Jack. Be with us soon enough.'

'Good work, so... Hold on! What the feck is he doing in Waterford? It's miles away.'

'Who knows?'

'I'm beginning to think it wouldn't be so bad if the fellas on Anglesea Street came down after all. Do we know how much he took?'

'A grand.'

'A grand? I didn't think they paid out as much as that.'

'They do if you ask nicely. Oh, and it was used in a store nearby, too, about the same time.'

'Do we know which one?'

'We do.'

'Right, get going, see if you can find a demented butcher or a surgeon who's been struck off, then get back here as soon as you. First thing tomorrow, we're away to Waterford.'

* * *

The Granville Hotel had, apart from the inevitable improvements dictated by the passage of time, changed little in three hundred years. With its stained glass windows, teak panelling and an abundance of Chesterfields, it managed to retain an air of subdued sophistication reminiscent of its past. Eamon's heels clicked across the marble floor as he approached the desk.

'Mr. Reilly, and how are you this evening, sir?' inquired the clerk.

'Oh, fine, so. This is me niece…'

'Of course she is, sir.'

Eamon hesitated, irritated by the insolent interruption, and drew a breath.

'I'll say that again.' He said, lowering his voice to a menacing level. 'This, is me niece. Would you care to see her birth certificate?'

'No!' said the clerk, blushing, 'I mean, Jesus, what can I say? I didn't mean…'

'Shut up. We'll be taking a drink or two. Now, if you've an ounce of decency in that pubescent head of yours, you'll apologise to the lady. Profusely.'

The clerk's head twitched erratically as his eyes looked for something to focus on other than Nancy.

'I'm so terribly sorry, Miss, really. I didn't mean to imply…' he said, fumbling beneath the desk. 'Please accept my apologies and take this, give it to the fella behind the bar, you'll have a couple of drinks on us. I hope. Sorry.'

'I bet you get that all the time,' said Nancy, sarcastically, as they ambled towards the bar.

'You have no idea how many nieces I have,' he said.

The bar, dimly lit and sumptuously furnished, was exactly as Eamon had described but, much to Nancy's dismay, was full to overflowing with overseas visitors intent on sampling every single malt available.

'Sorry,' she said, nervously, 'I can't go in there, it's too…'

'Enochlophobia?' said Eamon.

'What?'

'Fear of crowds.'

'Something like that.'

'Not a bother, would you like to go somewhere else? Maybe get a bite to eat? It's often quieter in the restaurant.'

'No, thanks,' said Nancy. 'I'm not that hungry. Really.'

'Are you sure, now? You look a little pale, have you not eaten today?'

'I had some breakfast.'

'Breakfast?' said Eamon, concerned for her welfare. ''Tis almost 8 o'clock, you'll be starving, so.'

Nancy smiled apologetically.

'Well,' she said, 'maybe just a sandwich.'

'Grand. Now, will we go to the restaurant, or…'

'I think, would you mind, could we go to your room? It'll be quieter, so.'

'Of course we can, if that's what you'd prefer.'

'I wouldn't want to impose, I…'

'Think nothing of it,' said Eamon, with a wink. 'I'd be glad of the company. Come so, we'll give room service a run for their money.'

The suite, on the third floor, overlooked the Suir and was simply but elegantly decorated. The street below, unlike Kinsale, which was often a-buzz with raggle-taggle tourists in search of a shamrock, was as calm as the river itself. Eamon hung his jacket on the back of the chair, took a seat at the table and perused the menu while Nancy shifted nervously on her feet by the window.

'There's a bottle of Jameson's on the side there, will we have a drink?' said Eamon.

'Please, thanks. That would be nice.'

'Why don't you do the honours and I'll see what delights the kitchen has to offer.'

Nancy filled a couple of tumblers with a generous measure of whiskey, sat opposite Eamon and handed him the glass.

'Sláinte,' she said.

'May your pockets be heavy and your heart be light,' said Eamon, raising his glass. 'Now then, Nancy, for some Godforsaken reason, it seems this hotel doesn't like to make anything with normal bread, they have these panini things, or maybe you'd prefer something a bit more substantial, a burger, perhaps?'

Nancy held the glass to her lips and gazed into space, her eyes dull, as though lost in thought.

'Nancy?' said Eamon.

There was no response. He placed the menu on the table, folded his hands beneath his chin and whispered as softly as he could.

'Cathleen?'

Nancy came to with a jolt, the colour drained from her cheeks as a look of dread crept across her face.

'Is it the tablets?' asked Eamon. 'I don't mean to pry, but there's a pharmacy up the road, if you tell me what you need I'll go fetch some. I really don't mind.'

She knocked back the whiskey.

'I don't know what you mean,' she said, rising to refill the glass. 'What did you call me? Who's Cathleen? Is that your daughter?'

Eamon, wary of inflaming the situation, stared wistfully at the ceiling and spoke as if overcome by a wave of nostalgia.

'Cathleen,' he said, 'was the wife I never had.'

Nancy turned and regarded him inquisitively.

'Is that so? What was she like?' she said.

'Oh, she was like yourself, really. Pretty, intelligent, funny, and not afraid to ask for help when she needs it.'

Nancy smiled.

'So, what happened?'

'The usual. Another fella. Bigger. Richer. Smarter. Swept her off her feet, so he did, off her feet and into his bed.'

Nancy's eyes glazed over.

'You really loved her, didn't you?'

Eamon hesitated, his voice croaking.

'I've never stopped.'

'You're a decent man, Eamon,' said Nancy, sympathetically. 'Heart of gold, so you have.'

'Then let me get the tablets. I'll not be long.'

Nancy pondered the suggestion.

'No, I don't think so,' she said, sternly. 'See, I've a problem, now.'

'And what's that?'

'You. You know about me. About me other name.'

Eamon, seeking to reassure her, smiled gently.

'Just so we don't get confused,' he said, softly, 'let me tell you something about names. As far as I'm concerned, you are Nancy. And I don't even know your second name. Cathleen is someone completely different. Cathleen is the girl who stole me heart, and there'll never be another. I'll say no more.'

Nancy moved behind him, put the glass on the table and gently rubbed his shoulders.

'It's a shame you never married,' she said. 'You'd have made a fine husband, so, and a good father too, I'm sure.'

'Well, it wasn't meant to be. Though not, I might add, for the want of trying.'

''Tis a shame.'

'Maybe,' said Eamon, 'but that ship has sailed, Nancy. I'll not dwell on it. What must be, must be.'

'That's right,' she said, her voice barely audible. 'What must be. Must be.'

Eamon had a hunch she wasn't about to walk out of the door and he knew, from experience, that to continue a conversation with someone in a state of depressed anxiety could easily make matters worse. Best, he thought, to let her get it out of her system, say her piece and then, if she wanted to, she could leave. He took a slug of whiskey, closed his eyes and braced himself for a barrage of abuse or, if it came to it, a couple of frustrated blows to the back of the head with a bottle of whiskey. There was neither. Just a faint rasping sound, like a razor coursing through dry stubble, as the serrated edge of the farmer's blade was drawn swiftly across his throat, its keen edge slicing effortlessly through his skin and beyond.

There was no pain to speak of, not immediately. He'd experienced worse from a shaving nick, until he gasped for air and realised there was nowhere for it to go. With his vocal chords severed, a garbled 'Hail Mary' tumbled from his trembling lips. His jugular, as efficient as a pump jack in an oil field unaware of the break in its circuit, continued to rhythmically spout blood from the wound, some of which travelled rapidly down the crisp, starched collar of his linen shirt, whilst the remainder flowed into his windpipe, causing him to cough and splutter like an old jalopy as he slowly began to suffocate, drowning in his own blood.

All at once, he grew faint and dizzy as his brain, starved of oxygen, robbed him of his senses until, as if succumbing to slumber, he slipped silently away. Nancy calmly returned to her seat, put the blade on the table and watched, entranced, as Eamon's face slowly turned a colder shade of blue. A muffled, gurgling sound, like water trying to escape a blocked drain, emanated from somewhere deep within his neck. She smiled, gently, as one would at a funeral, and crossed herself.

There was little that scared Nancy McBride. As someone with scant regard for her own well-being, confronting danger held no fear, but the unexpected sight of a dead man opening his eyes and glaring across the table, petrified her. The chair tumbled to the floor as she reached for the blade and lunged at the lifeless body, hacking and stabbing it about the head and neck in a furious frenzy until it collapsed in a bloody heap upon the table. A crimson tide oozed from the slash marks on his face and the gaping gash in his neck, gathering in a puddle beneath his chin before dripping lethargically to the floor. Eyes wide, her mouth dry, she paused to catch her breath and grinned maniacally, her heart pounding with a detached sense of excitement. Cautiously, she leaned forward, placed an ear as close as possible to his face and listened for a breath.

'Me uncle's sleeping, so,' she said as she breezed by the clerk on reception. 'I'll be back to fetch him at nine in the morning so don't disturb him, we've a busy day ahead.'

'Very good, Miss,' said the clerk, still harbouring some embarrassment from the incident earlier in the evening. Nancy stopped in her tracks, turned to face him and held up her left hand.

'It's Madam,' she said, wagging her ring finger. 'And don't you feckin' forget it.'

The bus, right on schedule, arrived in Cork just after 11.30pm. By the time the taxi had dropped her in Kinsale, it was a little after midnight. Against her better judgement, the call of the ATM outside the bank was impossible to resist. Without even bothering to look around, she pulled the card from her pocket, pushed it brazenly into the slot and confidently keyed in the number.

'Shite,' she cursed, under her breath, as the screen flashed up an unfamiliar message and swallowed the card. 'Feckin' shite.'

* * *

Two gold coins, sparkling in the yellow glow of the standard lamp, sat on the coffee table beside a bowl of murky water. Fearghus was dozing on the sofa. Beside him, feet up, was Brendan, out for the count and snoring loudly. Nancy lowered herself into the armchair and sat silently for a moment until, as though awoken by a sixth sense, Fearghus opened his eyes and smiled.

'What time is it?' he asked.

'Late,' said Nancy. 'Thought you'd be in bed.'

'Nah. We've not long eaten, excuse the mess, I'll clean up later.'

'Don't worry. What kept you up so late?'

Fearghus stretched his arms and yawned. 'The pen,' he said. 'We've finished the pen for the pigs, and we've built the ark, almost. Just the roof to go on. Me oul fella's worn out, so he is.'

'I'm not surprised,' said Nancy.

'He was up the river again this morning, came back and spent all afternoon and evening wiring up the fence. He's that tired, he didn't even take a drink.'

'I might now,' said Brendan, without opening his eyes. 'Nothing like a nightcap.'

Fearghus drained the last of the poteen and poured them all a dram.

'And yourself?' he asked. 'Did you have a good day?'

'Fair, I'd say,' said Nancy. 'You know Waterford, nothing much going on there.'

'Still, it's good to get out, change of scenery, so.'

'Here, I got you both something,' said Nancy, rummaging through her pockets.

'A souvenir? From Waterford?' said Brendan. 'I hope it's not another crystal decanter.'

Nancy pulled the farmer's blade from her pocket and tossed it on the table.

'Jesus! Have you hurt yourself?' said Fearghus, staring at the blood-stained knife.

'Oh, 'tis nothing,' said Nancy, hesitantly. 'Just nicked meself, so I did. Shouldn't be carrying it in me pocket.'

'Let me see. Are you alright?'

'Looks worse than it is, honestly, don't go worrying yourself.'

'But that's a lot of blood, are you sure…?'

'I'm sure. Here, Brendan, these are for you,' she said, hastily passing him the gloves. 'You'll not know the difference, though, you've hands like leather anyway. And here, as I've got your blade, you'll be needing something to replace it.'

Fearghus eyed the Leatherman.

''Tis a fine looking piece, you didn't have to.'

'There's lots of things I don't have to, but I do. I'm away to shower, you coming up?'

'Ten minutes. I'll finish me drink with Da and be along, so.'

Fearghus, glass in hand, nodded off as Brendan took the knife, held it gingerly between his fingertips and angled it towards the light. He studied it curiously. 'Must've been a hell of a nick,' he muttered to himself. Amidst the blood caked to the hilt, he noticed a couple of fine, greyish hairs and a few, tiny flecks of what looked like white cotton. He frowned, perplexed. Nancy's coat was brown, waxed, with a plaid lining. He sighed, heavily, and shook his head.

'Best give this a rinse,' he said, to no-one in particular. 'Wouldn't want it to spoil.'

Nancy grabbed the box from the back of the wardrobe, fumbled for the Tryptizol beneath the tissue paper and slipped a fresh strip into her pocket before stuffing the cash she'd liberated from the ATM, along with the Hudson City Savings card, into the folds of the dress.

CHAPTER 8

'Go back, again,' said Molloy, leaning on the desk. 'There, stop it there.'

Hanagan paused the footage from the CCTV and pointed at the grainy, black and white image.

'I'm telling you Jack, it's staring you in the face. Look at the time, there, there's no disputing it. That's the person who used Balducci's card.'

'No, no, no,' said Molloy. 'There must be something wrong with the clock, it can't be. She's a slip of a thing, too small and too female. She's not who we're looking for.'

Hanagan huffed, sat back in his chair and chewed the tip of his biro.

'Okay, then,' he said. 'Suppose you're right, suppose she's not the killer, but what if, what if she's working with someone else? Someone who is?'

Molloy stood up and stretched his back.

'You mean, she's just an accomplice, like?'

'Exactly.'

'Possible, I suppose. Can we track her movements when she leaves the bank, or see if there's anyone lurking about, kind of, waiting for her?'

'No chance. The only other cameras around there, belong to the tourists.'

Molloy grabbed the empty mug from his desk, passed it to Hanagan and gestured towards the kettle.

'Typical,' he groaned. 'Make it a strong one. So, we just wait, I suppose.'

'Say again, Jack, I don't follow.'

'We just wait, until the feckin' greedy, good-for-nothing uses the card again.'

'I'm afraid that's not going help,' said Hanagan. 'Not anymore.'

'How so?'

'The bank. Once we told them about Balducci, they closed his accounts. If anyone tries to use that card again, it'll get swallowed whole.'

'That's great, so. Feckin' great. I need to think.'

Molloy, his mind addled, sat and cradled his mug of tea, ruminating on the possibility that the perpetrator was not working alone. He shook his head in frustration.

'I don't buy it,' he said, slamming his mug on the desk. 'It doesn't sit well. It's giving me indigestion and I haven't even eaten, yet.'

'What is?'

'This whole accomplice thing. It doesn't make sense. If it's money they want, would they not simply rob him?'

Hanagan paused.

'Not necessarily,' he offered. 'She might not know what he's done. What if he robs the cards then gives them to her to get the cash out?'

'And how would she know the PIN number? No, we're looking for one fella. Mark my words, one fella who gets a kick out of seeing what people had for lunch, from the inside. Speaking of which, did you not find any deranged surgeons about the place?'

'No.'

'Any homicidal butchers on the loose?'

'No.'

'No psychos on feckin' day release?'

'That's a hat-trick.'

'Ah, well. Let's put it down as suicide, then. We'll say he was a contortionist.'

The phone rang.

'That'll be for you,' said Molloy.

Hanagan answered.

'I think not,' he said, holding aloft the receiver. 'It's the Garda in Waterford. They've another body.'

'Tell them we have one already.'

'They've heard about the contortionist, think we should go see theirs.'

Molloy sighed. 'Right, so. Tell them ninety minutes, if we don't get done for speeding along the way.'

They drove along Merchant's Quay, slowing to a crawl as they passed The Granville Hotel, its doors awash with blue and white tape, the pavement studded with Gardai.

'Would you look at that!' exclaimed Molloy. 'How many feckin' officers do they have up here? Anyone would think there'd been a murder. Drive on, park up the way there, we'll go see that fella in the store. Is it close by?'

'Closer than you think,' said Hanagan. 'We've just passed it.'

The salesman, dusting the remains of his breakfast from his tie, bounded forth to greet them, grinning optimistically at the prospect of a sale.

'Gentlemen! 'Tis a fine morning, is it not?'

'I've seen better,' said Molloy.

'Ah, cheer up, sure a fine looking fella like yourself has plenty to be grateful for. Now, is it a two-man tent you'll be wanting or something a little more, spacious?'

Hanagan held up his warrant card.

'Oh. You'll not be the outdoor type, then?' said the salesman.

'Oh, but we are,' said Hanagan, cheerily, 'we just don't enjoy it.'

'Will I get a chair?'

'This won't take long. Yesterday. A fella came by yesterday and bought something from yourself, about lunchtime, but he used a bank card you might not be familiar with.'

'Hudson City Savings Bank,' said the salesman, grinning like he'd won a prize. 'How could I forget? Sounds grand, does it not? Like something from the films, "Wonderful Life" or…'

'Could you tell us what the fella looked like?' said Molloy.

'Fella? It wasn't a fella. 'Twas a lass, a fine looking lass, on her holidays, so she was.'

'A lass?' said Molloy 'Could you describe…'

'Five-four, five-five maybe, lovely black hair, very pretty, late thirties, I'd say. I could tell she was the outdoors type by her hands. Weathered hands.'

'And she said she was on holiday?'

'Right so. Lived in America, place called Larchmont, I think it was.'

Molloy and Hanagan stared at each other in disbelief.

'Anything else?'

'No, I don't think so,' said the sales assistant. 'Oh, wait, she said she was a farmer, she and her husband.'

'Husband?'

'What did she buy?' said Hanagan.

'A pair of gloves and a Leatherman.'

'A what?' said Molloy.

'It's a knife.'

'Thanks, so,' said Molloy, grabbing his sergeant by the elbow and steering him towards the door. 'You've been most helpful.'

Molloy walked briskly back to the car and waited until they were seated inside before speaking.

'Are you thinking what I'm thinking?' he said, agitated.

'That Balducci was here with his wife?'

'Makes sense, does it not? They have a domestic, it gets out of hand, and then she tries to clear his account.'

'Gets out of hand?' said Hanagan. 'That's a hell of an understatement.'

'Well, she might have a history, you know, of being violent, like. Who knows, she might even have planned it, you hear about things like that. Anyway, chances are, if anyone knew his PIN number, she did.'

'If she planned it, there might be the odd insurance policy lurking about, too.'

'Insurance?' said Molloy, 'I like that, give us a lovely motive, so it would. Okay, here's the plan. I'll go see this fella in the hotel, you get back as fast as you feckin' can. I want Balducci's pals rounded up again, ask them, push them about Balducci, his partner, wife, girlfriend, whatever. While you're doing that, get someone to check with records in New York to see if he was actually married, then check if anyone using that name has booked themselves a flight or a boat trip out of the country.'

'Anything else?'

'What?'

'Nothing. So, you're thinking this fella, here, has nothing to do with Balducci, then?'

'I am, that. I'm thinking, and hoping, and I'm feckin' praying.'

* * *

Burglaries, assault and the inevitable Saturday night brawls comprised the bulk of Martin Fitzgerald's workload. If anyone expired on his patch they were invariably already in A&E as the result of natural causes or an overdose. Eamon Reilly was a casualty he could do without. Cold-blooded murders, particularly those where the victim was not intact, meant more paperwork, unpaid overtime, and blood. He hovered uneasily by the door to Reilly's room and toyed with a cigarette as the SOCOs and the pathologist went about their business. Molloy sighed as he ambled along the corridor, dismayed at the sight of his counterpart dressed in jeans, a navy blue bomber jacket and a black tee shirt. 'Wouldn't recognise a suit if he was lying in a feckin' coffin,' he mumbled under his breath.

'Molloy,' he said, sternly. 'I hear you've a fella with a headache needs looking at?'

'I have that,' said Fitzgerald. 'And it's not one a couple of aspirin's going to cure. Come so.'

Molloy squeezed past the inspector and, keeping his distance and his hands in his pockets, bent forward to get a closer look at the victim.

'Is this it?' he yelled back, without looking round. 'Sure, 'tis nothing but a flesh wound, should've seen the mess we had to clear up.'

Fitzgerald, on account of his weak constitution, remained wedged in the doorway.

'It's more than I can stomach,' he said. 'Put me right off ketchup, so it has.'

'Prefer the brown stuff, meself. Tom! This is a surprise!'

McKinley stood and stretched his gangly frame to full height. 'Hello Jack, if we go on meeting like this, we'll have to get a room, so,' he joked.

'No chance,' said Molloy. 'I don't like hotels, too feckin' dangerous for my liking. So, what brings you here?'

'Well, they thought, should there be a connection with this fella and the one you have at home, then I'd be the fastest way of finding out.'

'And is there? A connection, like?'

'So far, no, I'd say not, apart from the fact that he's not from these parts.'

'Not another tourist?' said Molloy.

Fitzgerald stepped inside the room and closed the door behind him, refusing to make eye contact with the corpse.

'No. He's not a tourist,' he said. 'Well, maybe, just a bit. His name's Reilly. Eamon Reilly. He was born in Sligo but the last forty years he's been living in Connecticut. He's got dual nationality. He was here on business, we think.'

'Do we know what?' said Molloy.

'His card says he works for Macy's, that fancy department store.'

'Anything else?'

'No. That's the odd thing about it, everything's as you'd expect to find it, apart from the fact he's had his head cut to pieces. It's like he was just dropped here from somewhere else.'

Molloy glanced around the room and made a mental note of the two glasses and the bottle of Jameson's.

'Anything missing?' he asked, turning to Fitzgerald, 'money, credit cards?'

'Not that we can tell. His wallet's full to overflowing, so it is. Plenty of plastic, plenty of cash. He still has his watch, too. Cartier, no less. I don't think we'll be using robbery as a motive.'

'Okay,' said Molloy, 'do me a favour, so, don't tell the bank he's dead, not just yet. Ask them to monitor any activity on his accounts, you know, debit cards, visa, that kind of thing. They may have been cloned or the details copied down. If they're used in any way we might be able use that information to track the perpetrator.'

Fitzgerald raised his eyebrows.

'That's genius, so! I'd never have thought of that.'

'Doesn't surprise me,' mumbled Molloy. 'What about a next of kin?' he added, more loudly.

'Waiting to hear back, but I've a feeling he was on his own. Nothing detailed in his passport and nothing in his wallet. Not even a photo.'

'Great. Well, thanks Martin.'

'Sure, anytime. Now, if you don't need me anymore, I'll be away downstairs. Those reporters will be wanting an update.'

Molloy wandered back to the table as the pathologist was packing up.

'So, Tom,' he said, 'do I have something to be worried about, or will I leave it to these fellas?'

'I'd keep an open mind, Jack. Two murders in a couple of days, there might be a link there, somewhere, but not in the way he was killed.'

'Go on.'

'Well, for a start, there's no murder weapon.'

'How thoughtless. Maybe he forgot.'

'Maybe,' said McKinley, smiling. 'Also, this wasn't the kind of blade you'd find in the kitchen drawer.'

McKinley gently lifted Eamon's head, taking care to support it with his left hand.

'Watch that doesn't fall off,' said Molloy.

'See the cut to the throat, 'tis slightly irregular, clean but irregular. Unlike the knife we found at your place, this blade had a serrated edge. Going by the depth of the cut and the wounds about the face and shoulders, I'd say it was about four inches long, four and a half, maybe, and an inch or so wide.'

'Could it be something like, like a Leatherman?'

'No.'

'Shite.'

'They're ten a penny, those things, and they're too small for a job like this. The blade on your average knife is about 1/16th of an inch thick. Whatever cut this fella had a blade double that. It'll be like a hunting knife.'

'A hunting knife?' said Molloy. 'Sure, there's no wildlife around here, except at closing time.'

'Exactly.'

'So, what do you think?'

'Well,' said McKinley, 'if I were you, Jack, I'd be looking for someone with something like, something like a farmer's blade, perhaps.'

'You've lost me,' said Molloy.

''Tis an all-purpose knife. Strong, high-tensile, steel blade used for cutting all manner of things, not to mention liberating the odd stone from a hoof or two.'

'And where would I get one of these farmer's blades?'

'Specialist shop,' said McKinley. 'I know of only one in Cork and one in Monaghan. That's it. Oh, and I'd say it was a fixed blade, not folding. You wouldn't get a pocket knife with a blade that size.'

'Would you draw me a picture, of what it looks like, be a great help, so it would.'

* * *

'You're back, so. How'd you get on?' said Hanagan, reaching for the kettle and a packet of Hobnobs.

Molloy tossed his jacket over the back of the chair, slumped in his seat and covered his face as he yawned.

'You first,' he said. 'And put a drop of whiskey in that, if we have some.'

Hanagan obliged and pulled up a chair. 'Well,' he said, dunking his Hobnob, 'I'm sorry to say our latest theory is crumbling faster than this biscuit. Oh, and Mrs. Molloy telephoned. She didn't sound too happy. Anyway, seems Balducci wasn't married, didn't even have a girlfriend. He was one hundred percent single, unattached and on his lonesome.'

'Is that so?'

'According to his mates, he wasn't great with the opposite sex, either, bit too handy with his fists, if you know what I mean. Apart from that, he was quite shy by all accounts, what you might call the retiring kind.'

'Shy?' said Molloy. 'He was American! You can't use the words "shy" and "American" in the same feckin' sentence.' He glugged his tea and gasped, 'did he have a record? For abuse, assault, against girlfriends?'

'No,' said Hanagan, 'well, nothing serious. A complaint or two, but that's all.'

'Ah, well,' he continued, ''tis good news, I suppose. Well, good and bad. Actually, it's all bad.'

'There you go with the riddles again,' said Hanagan.

'Let me enlighten you,' said Molloy. 'You see, Sergeant, it's bad because, had there been a relationship between Balducci and the mysterious lass with his credit cards, it would have made our lives easier because we might then have an idea of who we were looking for. But, as there's no relationship, we don't know how the feck she got her hands on his plastic, and, to cap it all, we have no idea what the feck she was doing in Waterford when this other fella happens to get killed.'

Hanagan rubbed chin as though it would improve the thought process.

'What if...' he began, 'what if Balducci picked her up without the other lads knowing? When he was on his own?'

'I doubt he'd have had the time,' said Molloy. 'Besides, you yourself said he and his mates were virtually in each other's pockets. Apart for the night he was killed.'

'That's it!' said Hanagan. 'The night he was killed! He left his mates behind, did he not, and wandered off alone? Maybe he went in search of... company.'

'What are you talking about?' said Molloy.

'Company. Female company. What if he was the kind of fella who was used to... well, you know, paying for his...'

Molloy frowned, shook his head and chuckled quietly.

'No. I really don't think so,' he said. 'I mean, where would you find one in Kinsale? If there was any prostitution around here, there'd be a queue outside the feckin' door.'

'Alright, here's another thing,' said Hanagan. 'We know Balducci wasn't married, right? And he didn't have a girlfriend. But, this lass told the fella in the camping shop she was from Larchmont. So, how did she know Balducci was from Larchmont, unless she'd met him?'

'Well, of course she'd met him, it stands to reason.'

'Yes, but what if she'd met him in Larchmont?'

Molloy groaned.

'That's the wife theory, only you've turned her into a transatlantic stalker and left out the insurance policy,' he said, rubbing his head. 'Something else doesn't add up.'

'What's that?' said Hanagan.

'Let's say she was, somehow, involved in the death of this fella in Waterford, too. Why wasn't he robbed? Why did she not take anything? His wallet was intact and he was still wearing his watch, Cartier, it was. If you ask me, it looks like he was slaughtered just for the craic.'

Hanagan downed his tea and stuffed an entire biscuit into mouth. 'I think you're looking for something that isn't there, Jack,' he said. 'Tom said the same about Balducci, remember? That robbery had nothing to do with it.'

'Right, so. He did that.'

'So, what about the fella in The Granville. Was it the same thing?'

'Worse, I think,' said Molloy. ''Twas nothing more than a simple case of having his throat slit. Plus, the odd stab wound, here and there. Oh, and his head was slashed to pieces. Looked like he'd washed his face in a food blender.'

'Is that all? So, how is that worse?'

'I don't know. Because there's no, no pattern, no… no continuity, and no murder weapon.' Molloy drained his mug. 'There was one thing, though. Whiskey. A bottle of whiskey and two glasses. There were a couple of cups at Balducci's place.'

'But no bottle.'

'Minor point.'

Hanagan stood and slowly paced the floor with hands clasped tightly behind his back. 'So, it seems to me,' he said thoughtfully, 'that the two murders might be related. But then again, they might not.'

Molloy raised his eyes to the ceiling. 'You're a feckin' natural, you know that?' he said. 'Carry on like this and you'll be Commissioner in no time.'

'So, is that it?' said Hanagan. 'Have we reached a dead end?'

'No. Not yet. We need to find a murder weapon. And, thanks to Tom, I have your next assignment.'

'It's not point duty, is it?'

'Don't tempt me. He drew a picture of the knife, or rather, what he thinks it looks like. See this, he calls it a farmer's blade. It's quite unique because of the size and the thickness of the blade, and there's only two places you can get them. Call them up and see if they have anything like it.'

Hanagan, frowned, puzzled by the request.

'Should the fellas in Waterford not be doing this? I mean, he was killed on their patch, wouldn't want to tread on their toes.'

'Don't you worry yourself, now. If there's a link between the two dead fellas, then this may be our only way of finding out. We'll have a chat with Waterford if we have to, now get going.'

Hanagan left the office and Molloy seized the opportunity for a few moments quiet contemplation. Leaning back, he closed his eyes and, as though lost in prayer, clasped his hands beneath his chin and tried to make sense of the facts. The mysterious girl from Larchmont troubled him. Almost as much as Mrs. Molloy.

'Shite!' he said, as he came to his senses and phoned home.

Brenda Molloy enjoyed being a housewife, she took delight in cooking and cleaning, washing and ironing, and talking all the while, like a worn record, about anything and everything but mostly nothing. In between talking, in an effort to lose weight, she'd spend her time at the leisure club or the walking club, then celebrate with her friends at the dining club and put it all back on again. Her favourite activity, however, was the two hours a week she spent at the cookery school, honing her talents as Ireland's most under-rated chef.

Molloy grimaced as she bellowed down the phone, ordering him to return no later than 6pm for his dinner, or all her efforts would be ruined.

'What?' he said, wincing as she bombarded his ear with gibberish. 'You've made what? What the feck is a rosti? You mean a potato cake? With what? A mousseline? Was he not a dictator? Oh, a celeriac mousseline, of course, I see. What the feck is celeriac? Can we not just have some chips instead? Hold on.'

Hanagan burst back into the office, waving a piece of paper and grinning like he'd won the lotto. 'Cork!' he whispered loudly. 'The fella in Cork thinks he made the knife, he'll wait for us, so, but we have to be quick.'

Molloy returned to his wife. 'I have to go,' he said. 'No, you don't understand, I've to go to Cork, official business, I've to see a man about a knife. No, I don't mean a dog, I mean a knife. I don't know, late. I'm sorry, so, but there's nothing I can do. Look, why don't you just eat for two? You usually do. Right so. Yes. No, the sofa will be fine. Bye, now.'

Molloy hung up, sighed with the consequences of a cordon bleu catastrophe and looked pleadingly at his sergeant.

'Have you ever eaten mousseline?' he asked.

'Don't be daft,' said Hanagan. 'You don't eat it, you put it in your hair.'

'She's trying to poison me, I'm sure of it. What's all the fuss?'

In an effort to coax Molloy from his chair, Hanagan pulled on his coat and spoke with a keen sense of urgency, eager to get moving as soon as possible.

'The shop in Monaghan only sells stock items, imported mainly and doesn't have any with a fixed blade, but the fella in Cork, the fella in Cork not only sells them, he makes them too, with his own hands. Quite the craftsman, so he is.'

Molloy heaved himself from his chair and knocked back the whiskey.

'That,' he said wearily, 'is what I call convenient. Where is he?'

'Plunkett Street, by the English Market.'

'Let's go. You drive.'

The sign above the shop read 'J P McCLEARY', the hand-painted letters, weathered and worn, had an antique feel about them but, in the absence of any description, gave no hint as to the trade of the proprietor. A black, metal grill, secured across the window for reasons of security, appeared to protect nothing more than a dozen or so empty display cases. Hanagan rang the bell.

'Hope we're not too late,' he said. 'Looks like he might have left already.'

'J.P.,' said Molloy, craning his neck. 'What's the J.P. stand for?'

'James Payton.'

'Payton? Now, there's a name you don't hear much these days. Grand, so it is.'

The door swung open and a short man, broad of shoulder, greeted them with a grin. His hair was cut in a short back and sides with the top as mad as a hedgerow. His ears seemed a little too large for his head and a willow pipe dangled from his lips. Molloy winced as his scarred hands shook his, crushing it with a vice-like grip.

'Molloy,' he introduced himself. 'Thanks for waiting. This is Sergeant Hanagan, he's the fella you spoke with on the phone.'

'Pleasure's all mine,' said McCleary. 'Come in, come in. I've some tea on, if you're in the mood.'

'Thanks,' said Hanagan, as they marched inside and settled by the well-worn, solid oak counter. McCleary, by the light of a single bulb dangling from the ceiling, poured himself a steaming cup of tea.

'You've nothing in the window,' said Molloy. 'Do you not…'

'Oh, I do, but I'll not leave me knives on display at night, not with all the scallies round here. They'd be through that window faster than a dose of Ex-Lax.'

'Fair point,' said Molloy, glancing around. 'You know, there's something old-fashioned about this place, reminds me of a sweet shop I used to visit as a kid. It's like nothing's changed in…'

'It hasn't,' said McCleary. ''Tis exactly as me Da left it. Some things in life are worth holding on to.'

'Ah, you're a man after me own heart, there. On the other hand, I have to say, sometimes it's nice to have a change, out with the old.'

'Like what?' asked Hanagan.

'Oh, like Mrs. Molloy, but that is a matter for the church to resolve. Now, then, Mr. McCleary…'

'James.'

'James. About the knife, would you look at this picture for me, now? We have to be sure, you understand?'

'Of course.'

McCleary held the sketch to the light and squinted as he studied it. 'Wait, so,' he said, and disappeared into the back room. Moments later he returned clutching a large box file and dropped it on the counter. Molloy looked on, noticeably impressed, as McCleary fingered through page after page of hand-written receipts and exquisitely detailed drawings of knives, the handles of which were intricately carved with traditional Celtic patterns.

'You draw these yourself?' asked Molloy.

'I do that. I have to know what it looks like before I can make it.'

'So you draw the pictures and you make them, too? Sure, you've more than your fair share of talent. The only thing I can draw is the curtains.'

McCleary smiled. 'Try something else,' he said. 'Maybe drawing's not for you. Have you not tried sculpture, perhaps? Or gardening?'

'Gardening?'

'Sure, why not? Takes a lot of skill, planning a nice garden, the layout, the colours, knowing what will grow in the shade and flourish in the sun.'

'Right, so,' said Molloy. 'Never thought of it like that. Might get meself a window box on the way home.'

'Ah-ha. I think this is what you're looking for,' said McCleary, as he pulled out a couple of sheets of A4 stapled together in the top left-hand corner. 'Jesus, time flies, so it does, it's almost ten years since I made that.'

'Ten years?' said Hanagan. 'How the feck can you remember that far back?'

'Easy. In all that time I must've made only four or five knives like that.'

'Is business that bad? Perhaps you should consider making forks, too.'

McCleary grinned. 'I mean, four or five knives with a blade that size, and only one with a serrated edge. Most people want a blade that folds, so they can carry it round without stabbing themselves in the hand. And here,' he said, turning the sheet over to reveal a Polaroid, 'is a wee photo.'

Molloy studied it by the light of the window. 'Maybe it's just a scratch on the photo,' he said, 'but it looks like there's something on the blade, some writing, maybe.'

'That's right,' said McCleary. 'The fella who bought it wanted it engraved. It was gift like, can't remember exactly, his son, maybe.'

'I don't suppose, I mean, I know you're not the memory man, but can you…'

'I can't, I'm afraid,' said McCleary. 'Me memory's not that good, but don't worry, so, I have it written down. Here we are, McBride. Brendan McBride. He has a farm, out towards Ballinacurra.'

Molloy grinned. 'You've just made an old Garda very happy,' he said as McCleary handed him the receipt.

CHAPTER 9

A brisk south-westerly hurled a handful of calamitous-looking clouds across the darkening sky as Fearghus, oblivious to the impending storm, watched his pigs devour the feed from the trough. Nancy, arms folded against the wind, ambled over to join him and nestled snugly beneath his protective arm. They stood silently for a moment or two and savoured the spectacle.

'It's nice to see some life back in place,' she whispered.

'Aye, 'tis that,' agreed Fearghus. 'I've missed it.'

'Where's the sow?' she asked, smiling serenely.

'In the ark, resting, and who can blame her?'

'They look happy,' said Nancy.

'Like yourself. You were out for the count last night, you must've slept well.'

'I did, that. I feel grand for it, too.'

Fearghus turned his attention to the litter.

'Won't be long before they're all grown up,' he said, thoughtfully. 'Another six months and they'll be on their way. Funny thing is, I'm not sure now, if I could let them go.'

'Don't get too attached,' said Nancy, 'you made that mistake with the sheep. They're not kids, they're a source of income.'

Fearghus sighed and gazed out across the field.

'I know, but they're like kids, are they not? I mean, they need tending to, feeding, looking after.'

He paused. 'Have you not...' he said, hesitantly, 'do you not think, one day, you might want to, you know...'

Nancy shrugged his arm from her shoulders and stepped to one side.

'We've been through that, Fearghus, and the answer's no. If I'd wanted children, do you not think I'd have started breeding by now?'

Fearghus smirked as the first, heavy spots of rain began to fall.

'I suppose so, but it's not too late, you know, if you change your mind, like.'

'At my age? I've told you before, the only thing you'll be fertilising around here is the soil.'

'Don't be daft, you're young, so, you've plenty of time to...'

'I said no. End of.'

Fearghus pulled his cap down over his face and gazed blankly into the distance.

'I was thinking,' he muttered, 'after I've taken care of the bonfire...'

'What bonfire?' said Nancy.

'All that stuff we cleared from the barn, it's been sitting there for weeks.'

'Can't it wait?'

'No,' said Fearghus. 'I want to clear it, it's a feckin' eyesore. Anyway, after that, I thought I might go see that fella about the boar. This afternoon, maybe. She'll be coming into season again, soon.'

'Is that all you think about?' said Nancy. 'Are you deliberately trying to wind me up?'

'What?'

'Listen, if you're that desperate, you should forget about the farm and open a feckin' orphanage, you're obviously after something I can't give you.'

'I am not. I only said…'

'Stop it!'

'I only said I was going to see the fella about the boar. I thought you might come with me, spend some time together, just you and me, have ourselves some lunch, somewhere.'

'In this weather? Are you joking me? No, thanks, take Brendan with you.'

'He's left already.'

'Left? Where's he gone at this hour?'

'Dublin,' said Fearghus. 'To get his coins valued.'

'Christ, you're both as stupid as each other. A few rusty bits of metal and he thinks he's won the feckin' lotto.'

'Well, at least he's doing something constructive, something with his time, something he believes in. What are you doing?'

'Will you stop with the questions!' snarled Nancy. 'I have stuff to do, that's all.'

'Alright, Jesus, I only asked. What is it with you these days? You come out here not ten minutes ago, all smiling and lovely and now you're chewing me feckin' face off. Sure, you've more swings than a feckin' playground.'

Nancy fixed him with a steely glare.

'Don't wait up,' she snarled.

* * *

The waiting room, tinged with an air of mild disinfectant, was empty, the receptionist, away from her post and the door to the surgery, slightly ajar. Brendan tapped politely and peered inside. Michael Mulligan was slumped in his chair, head back, snoring loudly, a copy of The Angler's Digest lay open across his chest. Brendan knocked again, a little louder. Mulligan jumped and woke with a start.

'Brendan!' he said. 'This is a surprise! Come in, come in, take a seat, why don't you?'

'Thanks, Doctor. I hope I didn't wake you, you seemed to be dozing, there.'

'Ah, 'tis nothing but boredom, Brendan.'

'Boredom? But you're a GP, sure, there's plenty of folk must need curing about the place.'

'I wish that were true,' said Mulligan. 'Problem is, these days, everyone's too feckin' healthy. Must be all that sea air. The only time I get to see anyone is when they're confined to bed or about to meet their maker.'

'Is it really that bad?'

'Put it this way, if I were a business, I'd have gone bust years ago.'

'Sounds like you could use an epidemic,' said Brendan. 'You know, nothing serious, just a bout of the old flu or something, just to get them through the door, like.'

Mulligan smiled.

'I'd offer you a drink but we've nothing in, unless you fancy a drop of surgical spirit, though perhaps...'

'I'm fine really, just popped in on the off chance. I'm on me way to Dublin and...'

'And you need something for the journey? Is that it? For the travel sickness?'

'No, I'm not troubled by that,' said Brendan.

'What ails you then? Is it the old arthritis?'

'No.'

'Rheumatism? When you get to our age...'

'No.'

'How's the old heart? The blood pressure? Will I do a test for you?'

'Thanks, no,' said Brendan. 'I just...'

'Have you checked your cholesterol?' said Mulligan.

'My what?'

'Cholesterol. If it's too high, I've some statins I'll prescribe you. Great they are, brings it right down. Mind you, once you're on them, there's no going back.'

'I don't think so.'

Mulligan sat back and sighed, slightly exasperated.

'Well, I can't see why you've come,' he said. 'Sure, you seem to be perfect health.'

'Advice,' said Brendan. 'I just wanted to tap your brain, like, if you have a moment, that is.'

'I'll check me diary. What do you think?'

'Grand. Now, the thing is this. I was coming home the other day, I'd been away, up to Whitecastle…'

'What for?'

'Doesn't matter. Anyway, I was coming down the lane and just got to me gate, when I saw this lying in the road. Now, I can't abide litter, as you know, so I picked it up, thinking I would throw it away, later, but then I read the back and I got curious, cos I've never heard of it. So I thought, as I was passing, on me way to the station, like, I'd drop by and see if you might know.'

Brendan pulled a foil-backed, plastic strip from his pocket and passed it to Mulligan who, through half-rimmed spectacles perched on the end of his nose, scrutinised it like a priceless antique.

'Interesting,' he said.

Brendan shuffled in his seat, uneasy at the ensuing silence.

'I was worried,' he said, 'you know, thinking, maybe, the animals might've eaten them.'

'No need to worry on that score,' said Mulligan. 'They can't get through the foil on account they have no fingers. And you found this in the lane, you say?'

'That's right. Well,' said Brendan, 'let me think… It was probably nearer the gate, just inside the gate.'

'The gate?'

'Maybe, nearer to the house.'

'The house?'

'The kitchen. I mean, I found it in the kitchen, by the bin.'

'I see,' said Mulligan, 'and you think, maybe, Fearghus, or…'

'I don't know,' said Brendan. 'I was worried, like…'

'No need to worry. It's Tryptizol, 50mg dose.'

'I know, Michael, I can read. But what's it for?'

'Tryptizol,' said Mulligan, as he removed his spectacles, glad of the opportunity to divest some medical knowledge, 'is just the brand name. It's basically Amitriptyline. 'Tis sometimes prescribed to treat headaches, severe headaches, migraine and the like.'

'And that's it?' said Brendan, staring at the doctor. 'That's not it, is it?'

'Well, to be honest, it's more commonly used to treat depression, manic depression. Though, why anyone around here would be depressed, is beyond me.'

'You need to get a few farmers on your books. Are they dangerous?'

'No, not if taken correctly, but an overdose could be fatal.'

'So I've nothing to worry about? They're safe, then?' said Brendan.

'I'd say so, apart from the side effects.'

'Side effects?'

'It depends on the individual,' said Mulligan. 'There may be some confusion, the inability to concentrate, plus a loss of libido, you know, the old sex drive, and it might impede the speech. More seriously, it could trigger episodes of a more, a more psychotic nature.'

'What does that mean?'

'Mania, delusion, hallucinations.'

'You mean, like a, like, what's the word? Like a skits-o-feckit?'

'Schizophrenic. Yes, broadly speaking, a bit like that. Only it's not long term, comes and goes.'

'Well, I've not seen anything like that, so it must be for the old migraine, then. Sure, I'm worrying over nothing.

You're a clever man, Michael, I might come down more often, just for a chat, like, been interesting, so it has.'

'Me door's always open, Brendan. Except when it's closed. Are you sure I can't give you something?'

* * *

Hanagan, as though deriving some sort of sadistic pleasure from seeing his boss mildly incapacitated, grinned as Molloy, groaning, lowered himself into his chair.

'You're late,' said Hanagan. 'Have you a problem with your back?'

'That sofa's too feckin' small for a fella like meself.'

'Sofa?'

'Don't laugh. You've this to look forward to. It's what they call "marital bliss".'

'I'll get you a coffee.'

Molloy winced as he struggled to find a comfortable position in sit in. 'Do me a favour,' he said. 'When you've finished with the racing pages, look through the Yellow Pages and see if there's a chiropractor nearby, I think me back's about to go.'

Hanagan laughed.

'Are you going soft in your old age?' he asked. 'Was a time you wouldn't go near anyone remotely associated with the medical profession.'

'That was me GP. Feckin' eejit he was. I went to see him because I thought I'd busted me foot. You know what he said? Eat white meat and practice yoga. He was lucky I didn't practice kung-fu, I can tell you.'

'You'll be fine, so,' said Hanagan, passing him a coffee and a couple of tablets. 'Here, paracetamol, they'll see you right.'

'Thanks,' said Molloy. 'So, what have you done this morning, apart from poring over the nags at Fairyhouse?'

'Actually, I've been busy, running checks on this McBride fella.'

'And?'

'Nothing. He's clean as a whistle. Married once, widowed twelve years ago, lives with his son and daughter-in-law on the same farm he grew up in. Not even so much as a parking ticket. I've a distinct feeling this line of inquiry is going nowhere fast.'

'Line of inquiry?' chuckled Molloy. 'You sound like a feckin' Garda. Well, I have to disagree, I have a hunch about this.'

'That's what Esmeralda said.'

'Who?'

'Nothing. So, what'll we do, then?' said Hanagan. 'Will we go see him?'

'We will,' said Molloy, as the phone rang. 'Just as soon as you've answered that.'

Hanagan answered and promptly covered the mouthpiece with his hand.

'Fella called Fitzgerald,' he whispered hoarsely. 'From Waterford. Says he's to speak with you as a matter of urgency.'

Molloy struggled from his chair, perched on the edge of Hanagan's desk, and took the call.

'Molloy speaking.'

'Jack, it's Martin Fitzgerald, there's something you should know.'

'Go on.'

'We've had a call from a fella who saw Reilly's picture on the television, said he saw him earlier in the day, in the pub, like.'

'And?'

'He was with a woman. Short, slightly built, black hair, wearing a waxed, cotton jacket. Sound familiar?'

Molloy groaned.

'Well, now, here's the thing,' said Fitzgerald. 'He swears blind he knew her, a lady by the name of Cathleen Moran, but she insisted her name was Nancy.'

'So? I don't see where this is…'

'Hold on. Cathleen Moran was interned at St. Dympna's; mental health issues. Apparently she killed a fella. Up in Kilkenny. Ten years back.'

'Oh,' said Molloy. 'And you're sure about this?'

'I am, that. The fella who saw her, in the pub, like, he used to work at the hospital, as a nurse. I've no reason to doubt him.'

'And he's positive? I mean, absolutely positive? Ten years is a long time. People change, so.'

'They do, I'll grant you that, but there's something else.'

'Go on.'

'Are you sitting comfortably?' said Fitzgerald.

'No. Just sitting.'

'We got two sets of prints off the glasses in Reilly's room. The results came back this morning.'

'This isn't going to be good news, is it?' said Molloy.

'One set of prints belong to Reilly, obviously. The others, I'm afraid to say, the others match the ones you lifted from the cup in The Blue Haven.'

Molloy's brow grew as furrowed as a freshly ploughed field.

'Thanks Martin. Appreciate it,' he said. 'I'll be in touch.'

Hanagan, eyes wide and mouth agape, eagerly awaited the news.

'Come on, then, Jack! What is it for feck's sake? You look like you've seen a ghost.'

Molloy heaved a sigh, stood and stretched.

'Well,' he said, 'despite what Tom thinks about Balducci's killer being a big, strong fella, seems we're now looking for a small, strong lass.'

'What? Who?'

'The lass on the CCTV. She's the only lead we have.'

'Lead? She's hardly that, Jack. We know she used Balducci's bank cards but as for her being in Waterford, that could just be pure coincidence.'

'Maybe,' said Molloy, 'and maybe not. They got a second set of prints from Reilly's room, they match the set we lifted from The Blue Haven,'

'Oh, shite.'

'And Fitzgerald has a witness who puts her in the pub with Reilly just a couple of hours before he was killed.'

'What? You're joking me?'

'I wish I was,' said Molloy. 'They reckon her name's Cathleen Moran and she was locked up for murder, in the mental hospital. See what you can find out, starting with St. Dympna's. If it turns out she's not involved, then, I'm sorry to say, we have absolutely nothing to go on.'

'Apart from the knife.'

Molloy turned to the window and stared out across the street.

'Maybe there's a link,' he muttered. 'Maybe there's a link between Balducci and Reilly. Maybe she's the link, but for the love of God, I can't see how. As soon as we get back, I want you to do some digging, and use a big, feckin' shovel.'

The rain eased as the car crunched along the gravel drive before coming to rest twenty yards from the front door. Hanagan eyed the weather-beaten farmhouse with envy. A couple of slates had slipped from the roof, the window frames needed a lick of paint and what constituted the garden needed weeding.

'That's what I call a house,' he said quietly. 'Not that pokey, plasterboard box I live in. Full of character, so it is.'

'If I lived there,' said Molloy, as plumes of white smoke billowed from the chimney, 'I dare say I could go the whole week without seeing Mrs. Molloy at all.'

'Sure, you've a nice enough place, yourself.'

'I have, that. Problem is, someone else lives there, too. Come, so, let's take a look.'

Hanagan cupped his hands against the window and peered inside while Molloy gave a couple of hefty raps on the door.

'No answer?' asked Hanagan.

'Can't be far, they've a fire burning. Let's look around the back.'

The gravel gave way to a muddy track riddled with puddles and potholes, which led them past an old stable block and on to an overwhelming view of rolling, green fields. A solitary figure, in a flat cap and pea-coat, was leaning, motionless, on a fence. He turned at the sound of their squelching footsteps.

'Tried knocking,' said Molloy, holding his warrant card aloft, 'but there was no answer. D.I. Molloy, and this is D.S. Hanagan. Do you have a minute?'

Fearghus, looking concerned, pulled his hands from his pockets and walked towards them.

'Is there something wrong?' he said, anxiously. 'Is it…'

''Tis nothing to fear,' said Molloy. 'Would you be Mr. McBride?'

'I am.'

'Brendan McBride?'

'No, that's me Da. What's up? What's he done?'

'Nothing, don't alarm yourself, now. We've just a question or two for him, nothing to be concerned about.'

'Don't tell me, he's double-parked again. Well, you'll not be seeing him today, I'm afraid. He's away, so.'

'Away? For how long?' asked Hanagan.

'Not long, he'll be back tonight. He's gone to see a numismatist, in Dublin.'

'A what?'

'A coin collector,' said Fearghus. 'Coin seller, to get something valued.'

'I see. Into the old metal detecting, is he?' said Molloy.

'No, not really. He found some old coins by the river, up near Whitecastle, he's gone to see if they're worth anything. Will we go inside? Getting a chill, so I am.'

Hanagan glanced around the kitchen, littered with the usual post-breakfast debris.

'In a rush this morning?' he said, sarcastically.

'It's a working farm, Sergeant, not a hotel,' said Fearghus. 'So, me Da's in trouble, is he? Better tell me what he's done.'

Molloy shook his head and smiled.

'No, he's not in trouble Mr. McBride, at least, we don't think he is. Would you take a look at this for me,' he said, pushing the Polaroid across the table, 'would you happen to know if your father has a knife like this?'

Fearghus picked up the photograph.

'Sure, no, but I have.'

'You have?'

'It was a present, a wedding present from me Da. Made special, it was. He even had it engraved, it's in the drawer here. I'll fetch it for you.'

Hanagan rose quickly as Fearghus reached for the drawer.

'Just a moment!' he said. 'Sorry, would you mind? I'd rather you didn't pick it up. May I?'

Fearghus stepped aside allowing Hanagan to retrieve the knife with the aid of a handkerchief. He frowned, perplexed at the sergeant's actions.

'What's going on?' he asked. 'Something serious, isn't it?'

Molloy stood.

'No,' he said. 'Not yet, anyway. We just need to… you know…'

'Can we borrow it?' said Hanagan, interrupting. 'Not for long. Let you have it back in a day or two?'

'I suppose so,' said Fearghus. 'But why would you be interested in…'

''Tis nothing really,' said Molloy. 'Don't you go worrying yourself now, we'll have it back soon enough. On your own?'

'Sorry?'

'Are you here, on your own, today?'

'Aye. Told you, me Da's away in Dublin.'

'And Mrs…'

'Oh, right, sorry,' said Fearghus. 'She's out too.'

'And when might she be back?'

'Christ knows. Mind of her own, so she has. You'll not be wanting her for anything, though, will you?'

'Oh, I doubt it,' said Molloy, with a smile. 'Formalities, maybe, that's all, you know how it is these days, have to double check everything.'

* * *

'So, what do you think?' said Hanagan, fastening his seat belt.

'What do I think?' said Molloy, wiping his forehead with a handkerchief. 'Well, we have the knife, we should be thankful for that, let's just hope it's the right feckin' one. Get it off to the lab like your life depended on it! No, better still, drop me at the station and take it there yourself, and tell them it's urgent. Tell them it's the most urgent job they've ever done. Understood?'

Molloy, hunched over his desk, held up his hand as Hanagan entered the office, fearful that his train of thought might be interrupted. He huffed and groaned and sighed with despair as he shuffled through a mound of papers like a teacher reading a particularly bad dissertation. Hanagan, apprehensive about moving, lest he should disturb his boss, shuffled nervously on his feet until Molloy finally lowered his hand, sat back and turned to face him.

'And where the hell have you been?' he asked. 'You've been gone for ages, were you doing the tests yourself?'

'Sorry, stopped off for a bite, I was starving, so. We've been on the go since…'

'Have you no sense of duty? There's a killer on the loose and all you can think about is your stomach.'

'Brought you back a sandwich. Two, actually. Bacon. Crispy. With the brown sauce.'

Molloy gave a crafty smirk.

'Dedication, that is,' he said. 'Glad to see you're not shirking your responsibilities, Sergeant. Now, hand them over, quick, I feel like I've been on a feckin' hunger strike. Tell me what happened.'

'They're on it,' said Hanagan. 'Reckon they'll have something in a couple of hours, and that was an hour and a half ago.'

'Good,' said Molloy. 'The sooner, the better.'

'So, what's up?'

'I borrowed your shovel and started digging. Seems Balducci and Reilly have about as much in common as the Pope and the Devil himself.'

'Well, there is... one thing,' said Hanagan.

Molloy stopped chewing.

'What's that?' he said quietly, anticipating a revelation.

'They're both dead.'

'Very helpful.'

'And,' said Hanagan, 'they're both single, neither had a next of kin and they were both, well, comfortably off, rich even.'

Molloy put down his sandwich and stared blankly at his sergeant.

'And you think the killer knew that?' he asked. 'You think she sat down and interviewed them, see if they ticked all the right boxes, before deciding to carve them up just for the hell of it?'

''Twas just a thought.'

'Stop thinking and pull up a chair,' said Molloy. 'I'm going to tell you about this Cathleen Moran, or Nancy, as she likes to be known. 'Tis quite a story.'

'Go on.'

'Her mother committed suicide when she was eighteen. Hanged herself. Found her dangling from the ceiling.'

'Ah, that's too bad,' said Hanagan. 'No-one should have to go through that. Do we know why?'

'No. She wasn't receiving treatment for anything and she wasn't on any medication. Came as quite a shock.'

'Bet it did.'

'A year later, coincidentally, almost to the day, she was done for murder, fella by the name of Mulligan, Dwight Mulligan.'

'Dwight?' said Hanagan.

'American. He was based at The Curragh.'

'Trying to learn a thing or two from our boys?'

'Something like that,' said Molloy. 'Anyway, one evening he and this other fella from the base were having a few pints in the pub, The Kyteler's Inn, and in walks this Cathleen Moran. According to the landlord, she was a total embarrassment. Starts out alright, just sits quietly with her drink, on her own, like, then she hears their accent, after that, she's over them like a rash. Especially this Mulligan fella, couldn't wait to get him home. By the time they left, they were completely ossified.'

'I've known a few girls like that, sure, they're out for the craic, that's all.'

Molloy frowned and shook his head.

'The craic is what he got, on the back of the head. She was found later that night wandering the streets, half naked, talking gibberish, mumbling to herself. When the Garda took her home, he found Mulligan on the kitchen floor, head caved in and a knife in his back.'

'Sure, she must be something else, this Cathleen, to take on a soldier?'

'That's why it's strange no-one believed her when she said it was self-defence. Claimed he'd raped her.'

'What? Did they not, you know, do the usual tests and stuff?' asked Hanagan.

'Apparently not. However, the investigating officer resigned two months later.'

'Why so?'

'Just as the case was about to go to court,' said Molloy. 'She miscarried. Lost the baby.'

'Shite. So she was raped after all. I'm feeling sorry for her now, she must've gone through hell.'

'After that, she became, well, withdrawn, introverted. Didn't speak, didn't eat. They say she hardly slept, spent most of the night wearing out the floor. The trial was postponed while she underwent a psychiatric evaluation.'

'And?'

'She got top marks. Manic depression. Her lawyer ran a defence of diminished responsibility and they dropped the murder charge. She was sent to St. Dympna's for manslaughter with a recommendation she serve no less than five years.'

Hanagan held his head in his hands and sighed.

'Make a great film,' he said. 'So, what happened next?'

'Ten years ago, almost, nine and a bit, she was discharged and disappeared without a trace.'

'What? No, surely not, I mean, she'd have gone home, would she not? They had her address.'

'The house was rented,' said Molloy. 'Once she was sentenced, the landlord sold off all her stuff and put the place up for rent again. She left the hospital alone and homeless.'

'It gets worse,' said Hanagan. 'Did the welfare not look after her? Make sure she was safe? Had somewhere to go?'

'Slipped the net,' said Molloy.

Hanagan sat back and gazed pensively at the ceiling.

'Orla Brady,' he said.

'What?'

'Orla Brady. She'd be great in the film.'

'Sometimes,' said Molloy, almost speechless, 'sometimes I… we need to find her. We need to find her and quick. I'll bet you a pint it's her prints on the glasses.'

The desk sergeant breezed through the door and handed over a large, sealed envelope.

'Just arrived,' he said apologetically. 'By courier, from the lab.'

'Grand,' said Hanagan. 'I'll announce the results in reverse order.'

'There's something else, Sir,' he said, looking at Molloy and lowering his voice.

'Go on.'

'Couple of fellas kicking off, out front. Say they're to see you right away.'

'Well, they can't. Tell them I'm busy,' said Molloy.

'They're from HQ, Sir. Anglesea Street. One of them has an awful lot of pips on his shoulder.'

'Shite! Keep them busy, tell them I'll be along, so.'

Molloy grabbed his coat and gestured for Hanagan to follow.

'Come, quick,' he whispered. 'We'll slip out the back way. Lively now!'

Hanagan, baffled by the urgency of their departure, parked the car a couple of streets away and regarded his boss in a state of confusion.

'Why the hurry?' he asked. 'Do they want something?'

'Of course they do. Answers. And this case. Open the envelope, let's see what we've got.'

Hanagan obliged and scanned the single sheet of A4.

'Okay, here we go. The knife's been cleaned, but only superficially, touch of the old Fairy liquid, couple of dabs. Identifiable but no match as yet, and…

'And what?' said Molloy.

'Bingo. DNA, matches our man Reilly.'

Molloy sighed and laughed softly, as though heading for a breakdown.

'At last,' he said. 'At last, we finally have a feckin' murder weapon. Right so, let's pick up the McBrides, both of them. About time we had a proper chat.'

'Hold on,' said Hanagan, 'Why pick up the McBrides? I thought we were looking for the girl?'

'We are,' said Molloy. 'And I think we've found her.'

CHAPTER 10

The rain eased to a fine drizzle and coated her hair with a diaphanous mist as she strolled aimlessly down St. John's Hill, cursing Fearghus and his litter of surrogate offspring as she went. She stopped at the bottom, her path blocked by an expensive, over-sized pushchair parked recklessly on the pavement outside a pretentious-looking shop called 'Moppet'. She pondered the consequences of pushing it into the street when a babygro, hanging in the window, caught her eye. She paused and stared longingly at the grinning monkey emblazoned across its chest and gently pressed a finger to the glass. Smiling, she stepped inside. The owner, in a crude attempt to up her sales, was fawning shamelessly over the owner of the buggy.

'Be with you in a moment,' she said, eyeing her with a look of distaste. 'Browse. If you must.'

Nancy glared at her contemptuously. She knew what she was thinking: that she could ill afford anything in the shop, that she was too old to conceive. Her eyes flashed fleetingly across the shelves and racks and glazed over at the sight of the babywear, the wooden toys and the sleepsuit with the smiling monkey.

'I'll come back,' she said, as she anxiously gnawed at her fingernails. 'I've somewhere I have to be.'

Slamming the door, she kicked the pushchair to one side and, as her eyes welled up, stormed off towards the river. She passed another buggy and a mother with a toddler before negotiating a screaming brood of tykes, their faces smeared with a mixture of melted ice cream and potato crisps. Her head twitched, as though afflicted by Tourette's, as her pace quickened to a jog. She ran, head down, oblivious to her surroundings, stopping only when she reached the bridge. She paused briefly, to catch her breath, then ambled across the Bandon and on to Castlepark.

The peninsula housed nothing more than a clutch of holiday homes, the sailing club and a pub, all within a hundred yards of each other. She passed them all, left the road and scrambled up the grassy slopes to the top of the isle and the ruins of James Fort. She dropped to the ground, sat with her knees pulled tight to her chest and stared out across the water. A trawler, flanked by herring gulls, pitched and yawed as it doggedly sliced its way through the black, choppy waters back to harbour. She lay down, arms outstretched and closed her eyes as the wind carried her thoughts out to sea. Within seconds, she was sleeping, sleeping and whimpering like a child tormented by nightmares.

Her breathing grew heavy and irregular, beads of perspiration peppered her forehead. A kaleidoscope of confused images hurtled round her mind, bouncing and merging in a multi-coloured theatre of mayhem: her mother, happy, laughing, then swinging gently by the neck from the light fitting in the front room, the stench of alcohol, a soldier, his face tainted by anger, bearing down on her, a small child, bewildered and confused, wandering bare-feet along a rain-sodden street, the bare, grey, concrete walls of a hospital room closing in on her, her feet in stirrups as a masked man probed and poked her most intimate parts with all the finesse and dexterity of a plumber trying to unblock a drain, and the sound of a baby crying, a young baby, desperate to be held.

She woke in the foetal position, her hands clammy, her clothes damp, intuitively aware that someone was watching her. She cautiously turned her head towards the sky and came face to face with a pair of large, brown eyes. Kind, sympathetic eyes set either side of a shiny, wet snout. The Labrador, its tail wagging with the regularity of a metronome, raised a paw in greeting. She took it and smiled as it drooled and panted with excitement.

'Bailey!' yelled a voice. 'Bailey, will you stop being so feckin' friendly! Leave the lady be, now.'

Nancy sat up, smiled and stroked him gently on the head.

'Bailey! I've told you before! Sorry, he's the inquisitive kind, I hope he didn't bother you.'

Nancy rose to her feet, pleasantly surprised at the unexpected intrusion, and shot the stranger a coquettish grin as she wiped her hands on the seat of her pants. There was a feral charm about him, something of a ruffian, tall and unshaven with a headful of black, curly hair that tumbled carelessly to his shoulders.

''Tis fine, really,' she said. 'He's a lovely dog.'

'He's just a youngster, but he's an eye for the ladies. Tinker, so he is. Anyway, like I said, sorry if we disturbed you. We'll leave you be.'

'No,' said Nancy. 'I mean, you don't have to go on my account. I was just, you know…'

The stranger regarded her quizzically.

'Actually, no, I don't know,' he said. 'I mean, there's nothing to do up here but…'

'Escape.'

'Escape? I was going to say "think".'

'That's what I meant,' said Nancy.

'Don't blame you. I do the same. 'Tis a great place to come and clear the old head, like.' The stranger held out his hand. 'Harry,' he said. 'Me name's Harry, Harry Malone.'

Nancy sat down again.

'Do you mind?' said Harry, pointing to a spot on the grass beside her.

'It's a free country,' she said coyly.

'Sorry, I don't know your...'

'Nan...' she began, before changing her mind. 'Cathleen. The name's Cathleen.'

Bailey sat beside her and rested his head on her knees.

'Someone likes you,' said Harry.

'Takes after his owner.'

Harry, clearly embarrassed by the flirting, laughed nervously.

'So, Cathleen,' he said. 'How's the thinking going? Are you okay? Your eyes, they're red, so. Have you been...'

'Probably. Just a bad dream, I think.'

'You're sure now? Cos I wouldn't want to intrude, if you'd rather we...'

'No. Stay, really. Could do with the company, I think. Sometimes, it's dangerous to be alone with your thoughts.'

'Penny for them?'

'They're not worth that much,' said Nancy.

'I don't believe it.'

'It was just, I was just thinking, about, stuff. A babbie. About the babbie.'

'Your babbie? Boy or girl?' asked Harry.

'Neither,' said Nancy, ruefully. 'She, it, decided it didn't want to come out.'

'I don't... oh, I see. I'm sorry. I...'

'It's fine. It was a long time ago, but sometimes stuff like that, it doesn't go away, does it? I guess she wasn't ready for this world. Still. Enough about me, how about you? Do you not have any kids?'

'Me? No,' said Harry, with a hint of regret. 'I have Bailey, though, and he's enough to...'

'You're not...'

117

'Married? No. Engaged? No. Girlfriend? No. And gay? No.'

Nancy giggled quietly and brushed a tress of hair behind her ear.

'I'm surprised, fine looking fella like yourself, you should've been snapped up years ago.'

'You're full of the old blarney, you know that?' said Harry, grinning.

'It's a gift, so. Come on then, what brings you here? You're certainly not thinking, by the looks of it.'

'Sure, I don't have time to think,' said Harry. 'Not at the moment, anyway. I look after the houses, behind the sailing club, there, where all the rich folk come to get a slice of Irish culture.'

'Culture? Is that what they call it?' said Nancy.

'Aye, but they're not into Yeats or Joyce, or Beckett or Heaney. Their idea of culture is Guinness and leprechauns and that feckin' Danny Boy.'

Nancy held a hand to her mouth and giggled.

'You're funny, so,' she said, glad of the light relief.

'Not really, just telling it like it is.'

An awkward silence punctuated their conversation. Harry, reluctantly, stood as Bailey barked, signalling it was time to move on.

'Well,' he said with a groan, as if standing was a strain on his back, 'we'd best be off. Bailey'll be wanting his lunch.'

'Okay,' said Nancy, as she pulled blades of grass from the ground, clearly disappointed.

Harry hesitated, unwilling to let the moment pass.

'Will you not... I mean... Would you care to join us? Me house is over the way, there, not far. And we've plenty to eat, if you don't mind a sandwich like, some cheese and some ham...'

'No, thanks, I shouldn't. You're a busy fella, it wouldn't be...'

'Sure, 'tis no trouble,' said Harry. 'I'm finished for the day, now, so there's nowhere I have to be. Cup of coffee, if you're not hungry? Look like you could do with warming up.'

Bailey barked.

'Alright,' said Nancy, offering up her hand. 'I'd like that.'

They trudged across the damp grassland, Harry, hands in pockets and Bailey bounding excitedly by Nancy's side. Before long, she caught sight of a ramshackle hut. It resembled an abandoned crofter's cottage, half timber, half stone, with a corrugated iron roof bolted precariously on the top.

'Would you look at that dilapidated old thing,' she said. 'I'm surprised that's not been blown away. Probably full of pigeons and all sorts.'

Harry smirked.

'That's me house you're talking about,' he said.

'You're joking me! Oh, shite, I didn't mean…'

'Don't you go worrying yourself, now. You're right, it could use a lick of paint, but I'll tell you this. That wee cottage has taken everything the sea can throw at it and it's still standing. Just.'

'It does have a certain, charm, I suppose,' said Nancy.

The small, open-plan cottage was cosy and warm with a wood-burner throwing out the heat. Rustic, book-lined shelves were screwed to the timber walls and a large, dining table fashioned from shipping pallets sat beneath the window.

'Not to everyone's taste,' said Harry, as he held the door open. 'It's a bit basic, but…'

'Basic?' said Nancy with a grin as she surveyed her surroundings. 'It's feckin' 19th century. It's like something out of that Little House on the Prairie.'

Harry tossed his jacket to one side, grabbed Bailey's bowl and filled it with a handful of chicken and rice.

'I'm a simple man,' he said. 'Uncomplicated. Not what you might call, materialistic. Besides, I've everything here any new house has. Hot water, electricity and, would you believe, a flushing toilet. It's just wrapped up in a different package, that's all.'

'That's lovely.'

'What is?' said Harry, frowning, as he scoured the shelves, trying to figure out what she had seen.

'What you said. You've a way with words, so you have.'

'You're a one, you know that? Now, we've tea or coffee, the ham or the cheese, tomatoes or onions or, a bit of the old pickle, if you're feeling fruity, that is.'

Nancy, as infatuated as a schoolgirl, sat on the well-worn sofa next to Bailey.

'Bet you've said that a fair few times,' she said.

'You'd be surprised,' said Harry. 'At how little, I mean.'

'Ah, go on, I bet there's been many a lady sat where I'm sitting now.'

'That's where you're wrong. I have a sixth sense when it comes to, entertaining.'

'Is that so?' said Nancy.

'He's called Bailey. Good judge of character, so he is, if he doesn't like someone, there's a reason why. He's taken to you though, so I must be in safe hands.'

'Now, who's doing the flirting? So, you're on own then? A bit of a loner, are you?'

Harry laughed and passed her a cup.

'You mean, like, the mad fella who carries an axe and never goes out?' he said. 'No, but I like me own company. I'm comfortable in me own skin, I can do without all that gossiping and socialising and drinking til you fall over stuff. The folk who do that, they're afraid of themselves.'

Nancy sipped her coffee.

'Is there something in this?' she asked.

'Just a dram,' said Harry. 'Keeps out the cold.'

Nancy gazed pensively towards the ceiling.

'You know something? If you'd have told me this morning I'd be spending the afternoon with an intellectual hermit, perched on the edge of a cliff, philosophising about the social classes, I'd have said you were a spud short of a pound.'

Harry nudged Bailey from the sofa and sat beside Nancy. She pulled her knees up and turned to face him, inching just a little bit closer, and studied his roguish features.

'What is it?' she said, softly.

'Sorry?'

'There's something on your mind, I can tell.'

Harry looked into his cup and smiled.

'Well, if you don't mind me asking,' he said. 'I mean, if you don't want to talk about it, that's fine, but you mentioned, you mentioned a babbie. I was just thinking, it must've been tough. Was your husband not, I mean, did it not affect him, like it..?'

'Husband?' said Nancy.

'Aye,' said Harry, 'well, I saw your ring, I just assumed...'

'Ah, pay no heed to that, 'tis just for show, wards off the undesirables, so it does.'

'So, you're not married then?'

'Oh, there's been many a fella missed his chance of eternal bliss with meself, but it's their own fault.'

'How's that?'

Nancy grinned.

'Too much... socialising. And drinking til they fell over.'

She smiled contentedly as the conversation paused and the air filled with the subtle sounds of Bailey snoring, the logs hissing and the radio warbling gently in the background.

'This is nice,' she said. 'It's so peaceful here, so, relaxing.'

'There's nothing like it,' said Harry, topping up their cups with another shot of whiskey. 'There's a lot to be said for being a loner.'

'Listen,' said Nancy, as she cocked her head to one side. 'On the radio, "Valley of Slievenamon". I've not heard that in years.'

'You're showing your age, now.'

'You've a cheek,' said Nancy. 'I used to love listening to that. And dancing. I used to love dancing the waltz.'

'We could dance now, if you like,' said Harry.

Nancy, taken aback, watched with delight as he stood, placed his cup on the table and held out his hand.

'Come so,' he said. 'May I have the pleasure?'

Bailey raised his head and looked on with an air of indignation as they whirled carelessly around the confined space, smiling bashfully at one another. Their dancing slowed as they drew closer and the waltz gave way to a rasping rendition of 'A Rainy Night in Soho'. Swaying slowly in each other's arms, Nancy drew herself up on tip-toe and kissed him gently on the lips.

'Well,' said Harry. 'That's not what I expected. I could do with a drink.'

'Not for me,' said Nancy. 'If I have another I may do something stupid.'

She winked, held out her cup and knocked back another tot. Smirking, she began unbuttoning his shirt. He raised a hand and placed it on hers.

'Wait,' he said, quietly, 'not here.'

'What?'

'Not in front of Bailey. I couldn't.'

He led her to the bedroom. It was small and sparsely furnished, with no door and not much more than an old chest of drawers and a huge, cast iron bed covered in a patchwork quilt.

'Where the feck did you get that?' she said. 'Grandpa Walton?'

''Tis the most comfortable bed you'll ever lie in.'

'I'll not take your word for it,' she said, pulling her sweater over her head. 'I want to find out for meself.'

A framed photograph on the bedside table caught her eye. A small, blonde boy gripping a bucket and spade, grinned back as she eyed it with a look of revulsion.

'Who's that?' she said, brusquely, a nauseous wave rising in her belly.

'What?' said Harry. 'Who's who?'

'Him! You've a boy, that's your feckin' son, isn't it?'

Harry threw his head back and laughed.

'No, no, it's…'

'What's so feckin' funny?' screamed Nancy. 'All this time you've been spinning me a yarn. No wife, no children, you said. You feckin' lied to me! You feckin'…'

'Whoa! Hold on, there,' said Harry, raising his hands. 'I was about…'

'Just another chancer. You're full of shite! I should've known!'

'Will you quiet yourself!' said Harry. 'Listen, I've no idea who the boy is. He was in the frame when I bought it. I've a snap of Bailey to go in there, look, here, see.'

He snatched a photo from the chest of drawers and passed it to her.

''Tis grand, is it not? Look at the fella, sleeping, with his legs crossed.'

Nancy grimaced, raised her eyes and looked at Harry forlornly.

'Sorry,' she whispered. 'I'm such a fool, I don't know what came over me.'

Harry wrapped his arms around her and gave her a bear hug.

'Nothing wrong with making a fool of yourself,' he said. 'But you could do with some anger management, you've a rage in you, so you have. Hope you're not like that in bed.'

Nancy grinned and thumped him playfully on the chest.

'I'm worse,' she said, as she finished unbuttoning his shirt.

She threw her arms around his neck, kissed him again, and forced him onto his back.

'Hold on,' said Harry, as she lay on top of him. 'Do you not think, do you not think this is moving a bit fast? I mean, we've only just met.'

'So what?'

'Well, call me old-fashioned but, I like to court a girl, you know?'

'You can court me afterwards,' said Nancy.

'So, is this like a one-night stand, then? Only in the daytime?'

'I hope not. Besides, I've never known a fella turn down the chance of a… you know.'

'Then you've not met the right fella.'

'Oh, I think I have,' said Nancy. 'Who knows, you might be the one.'

'The one?' said Harry.

'Sure, the one who gets me pregnant.'

Harry's jaw dropped in bewilderment.

'What? Now, hold on, just a minute, there, Cathleen, I'm not sure about this, what are you? Some kind of black widow?'

Nancy grinned mischievously.

'I'm joking you,' she said, jumping from the bed. 'Wait there.'

'What? Where are you…?'

She returned wearing nothing but her underwear with Bailey's leash wrapped around her fist.

'What are you doing with..?'

'He'll not need it for a while,' she said. 'I'm just borrowing it.'

'Are you one of those kinky…?'

'Ah, 'tis just a bit of fun. Gets me going, like. Come on, turn over, it won't hurt.'

Intrigued, and somewhat aroused by her antics, Harry obediently rolled over, allowing her to bind his wrists behind his back. He yelped as she pulled it tight.

'Steady on,' he said, laughing.

'Right, so. Turn over.'

'This isn't exactly comfortable,' said Harry.

'It's not meant to be,' she said, biting her lip as she unzipped his fly.

'Listen, Cathleen, I don't mind a bit of fun, but I don't think we should, you know, go the whole way.'

'And why's that?' said Nancy, in a lilting tone.

'Well, I told you, we've only just met, and anyway, it's been a while, I've no... you know, protection.'

'And you're worried you might get a little over-excited, is that it?'

'Probably,' said Harry. 'Look, I don't... I just don't want to get you pregnant, that's all.'

There was a moment's silence as Nancy, unbuckling his belt, paused and looked away. She frowned, as if distracted by a distant conversation, and gave his jeans a hefty tug.

'Is that so?' she said, addressing the ceiling. 'Well, 'tis me who'll be pregnant, not you, so don't you go...'

'Cathleen, this is silly. Come so, untie me...' said Harry.

The look in her eyes unsettled him. The sparkle had gone, in its place, a hollow, vacuous stare, as though her mind was elsewhere. She took Bailey's collar and, despite his best efforts to avoid it, placed the thick, leather strap gently around his neck. An impish smile returned to her face.

'Are you rejecting my advances, Mr. Malone?' she said, playfully. 'How's that? Too tight?'

'No, I'm not rejecting... it's fine. No, it's not tight.'

The smile suddenly faded from her face.

'Am I not pretty enough? Is that it?' she scowled, tightening the collar.

'You're feckin' gorgeous,' said Harry, 'but look, you've had your fun, now loosen it will you, it's making me...'

She paused, glowering at Harry as though she'd been betrayed, wronged, spurned. Her lip curled in disgust. She leaned forward.

'Am I too old?' she snarled.

Harry, gasping for air, threw his head back as she yanked the collar as hard as she could.

'Jesus, woman!' he wheezed 'I can't breathe properly! Take it off, Cathleen, take it…'

The buzzing in his ears was loud enough to block the sound of Nancy's grunts and groans as she jerked and pulled the collar tighter and tighter, gritting her teeth as she struggled with the effort. The buckle dug deep into his neck, bruising his throat while his eyes, bloodshot and bulging like a couple of soft boiled eggs, threatened to pop from his head. His arms twitched spasmodically behind his back as his sinuses closed up, until, as though faint from hunger, his dizzy, cloudy head lolled back and a stillness descended upon him. Nancy held her breath for a count of sixty. Her shoulders slumped as she sighed with relief and released her grip. She gazed down at his pallid face, his wide, red eyes, and smiled softly, brushing the hair from his forehead and humming 'Slievenamon' as if it were a lullaby.

The room darkened as the sun began to set, casting a shadow across his sculpted face, his boyish features transformed into the chiselled effigy of a detestable, uniformed misogynist. Reviled by the sight of his perfidious lips, she wiped her mouth, raised her hand and brought her fist crashing down against the side of his face. His head rolled with the force of the impact, his cheek, smarting from the blow, flushed instantly.

Picking chunks of cheese from the uneaten sandwiches, she watched from the window as a barrage of murky, grey, storm clouds rolled slowly towards the mainland. Enveloped in the tranquility, she wrapped her arms around her naked chest and closed her eyes, her hips swaying like a sapling in the breeze to a tearful lament drifting from the radio. It wasn't the rumble of distant thunder that shattered the peace, nor was it Bailey's bark that caused her to jump. And it wasn't the flash of lightning that made her scream with terror.

* * *

'Are you feckin' crazy?' Harry yelled, as he hurried unsteadily towards her, his hands still bound behind his back, his eyes reanimated with a red, raging fury.

The plates crashed to the floor as she spun around, trapped between Harry and the table. Petrified, she fumbled furiously behind her back in a desperate search for something to defend herself with.

'Keep away from me!' she cried.

'Untie me, you feckin' psycho!' boomed Harry, as he loomed towards her. 'You nearly feckin' killed me! I nearly feckin' choked to death!'

Bailey, as playful as any dog, barked and bounced excitedly about the sofa as Nancy screamed and lunged at Harry, slashing his face with the breadknife, its keen, serrated edge carving a bone-deep gash across his cheek. He reeled from the force of the blow, twisting and toppling to the floor, swearing and cursing as the blood flowed freely down his face. He winced, caught his breath and tried stoically to struggle to his knees, failing and flinching as she struck again, the knife slamming into his shoulder like a machete slashing a melon.

Exhausted, he slowly raised his head and gazed into her fiery eyes with a look of bewilderment. She huffed indifferently, forced an apologetic smile and took a final swing, ripping the blade across his neck with a single stroke, tearing through the jugular and rendering him speechless. She cringed, then smiled as a shot of warm blood spurted against her naked thigh and trickled down her leg. She watched as he wavered and teetered like a drunk defying gravity, annoyed that he wouldn't fall over. She gave him a shove, a short, sharp shove with her foot and watched, gleefully, as he collapsed in a heap, his head landing with a dull thud. Chest heaving, she grinned and dipped a toe in the sticky, scarlet puddle beneath his chin while Bailey, assuming that the game was over, sought out his reward and devoured the sandwiches beneath the table.

As night fell, and the wind whistled over the roof, she scrambled for her clothes, desperate to leave, anxious that someone might call unexpectedly, someone from the holiday homes or someone related to the boy in the picture frame. She fastened her coat and rifled through the pockets, looking for the Tryptizol. Instead, she pulled out a tiny romper suit, stared at the smiling monkey, and tossed it into the stove.

Although the threat of rain had passed, the low, thick cloud remained, making it darker than usual, too dark for any sane person to be wandering alone at night, too dangerous for anyone in their right mind to be traversing the slippery, grassy knoll back to the sailing club. She was glad to have Bailey by her side.

CHAPTER 11

It was the kind of smell one grew accustomed to, offensive to some, accepted by others. Fearghus, scraping his boots with a wire brush over a token sheet of newspaper on the kitchen floor, was oblivious to the pungency of the odour. He paused for a moment and took a swig of coffee as the front door slammed down the hall. He could tell by the footsteps it was not his wife.

'Da!' he said, as Brendan shuffled wearily through the door. 'You made good time.'

'Just as well, lad, looks like a hell of storm coming, and there's a fair old wind blowing behind it.'

'It'll pass, I'm sure.'

'I doubt it, and talking of a wind blowing, what the feck is that smell?'

'Smell? Oh, I'd say it's the pig shite on me boots. It's not that bad.'

'That's where you're wrong, lad. Don't light a match and for Chrissakes open a window. Where's the lovely Nancy?'

'Out. Still.'

'Then count your blessings and get that lot cleaned up before she gets back. You know what she's like.'

Fearghus, not one to willingly incur the wrath of his wife, nor his father, fetched the broom and swept the toxic debris out the door.

'How long will she be?' asked Brendan.

'How would I know?'

'But it's your anniversary.'

'Don't remind me,' said Fearghus. 'I've a ring in me pocket, should've given it to her this morning, before she…'

'Before she what? You didn't argue again?'

'She took herself off before I had a chance to, you know, patch things up.'

'I'll not ask what it was about, that's private business, between you and her.'

'Thanks. So, how'd it go?' said Fearghus. 'Did you see the numismatist?'

'I did, that. And I've some news for you. Good news. Come, sit.'

'I've some news, too. Only, it's not so good. Who'll go first?'

'You, but judging by the look on your face. I dare say we'll be needing a drink.'

Fearghus fetched a couple of glasses and a bottle of whiskey, joined Brendan at the table and poured them both a large measure.

'Right,' he said, 'ready? This morning, we had a visit.'

'That's nice.'

'The police.'

'Not so nice. What the feck did they want? Probably some Garda bored out of his…'

'No, Da, wasn't a Garda, they were detectives.'

'Detectives?'

'Two of them. They were asking for you.'

'Me?'

'And they took me blade, the one you gave me.'

'Why on earth would they be taking the blade? Sure, it makes no sense, I...'

Brendan paused as he remembered cleaning the knife the night Nancy returned home late, washing away the blood, Nancy's blood.

'What?' said Fearghus. 'What is it?'

'Nothing,' said Brendan. 'Forgot what I was going to say, that's all. What else?'

'That's it. Said we could have it back in a day or two.'

'What? Did they not say why they wanted it? Or give a reason for taking it?'

'No.'

'And you didn't think to ask?'

'Well, I...'

'Taking the knife is one thing, but why would they be asking for meself?'

'I don't know,' said Fearghus. 'You haven't been out slashing tyres or something, now, have you?'

'I'll slash you in a minute.'

'Hold on, they had a photograph, of the knife. Got it from a fella called... McCrear...'

'McCleary?' said Brendan.

'That's it.'

'Sure, he's the fella who made it.'

'Well, maybe something's happened to him.'

'That'll be it, but frankly, I don't care. To be honest, I've too much to think about. Can't be wasting me time with a couple of peelers asking after nothing. Did they give you a receipt? Some of that lot have very light fingers and regular bouts of the old amnesia.'

'They did not, but I'm sure it's fine. They seemed like regular fellas.'

'Well, no doubt, if it's important, they'll be back. Now, you best top up these glasses and brace yourself.'

Fearghus poured another dram and watched his father knock it back in one.

'So?' he said. 'Don't keep me in suspense.'

'Those coins,' said Brendan. 'The gold coins, the Commonwealth coins. Seems they have a value after all.'

'That's great, Da! I'm glad to hear it, amount of time you've spent sifting through all that silt, getting soaked to the skin, sure, you deserve it. Come on, then, what did he say? Fifty each? A hundred, maybe.'

'Maybe. And maybe a bit more.'

Brendan folded his hands on the table, leaned forward and stared his son in the eye. 'Five,' he said quietly.

'Five hundred?' said Fearghus, excitedly. 'That's grand, Da! Well done!'

'Five thousand.'

'What?'

'You heard.'

'Five thousand?' said Fearghus. 'Each? Jesus, Mary and Joseph! How, how many do you have?'

'I daren't count. More than ten. Twelve, maybe, fourteen.'

'I don't know what to say.'

'Say nothing. I'm to see him in a day or two. If he's happy with the others, he'll give me a cheque, so, your troubles are over, son. You need worry no more.'

'I can't believe it! Just wait til I tell Nancy. She'll be… No, hold on, Da. They're your coins. I can't be taking that money from you. Besides things are on the up, we'll be fine, soon enough, once…'

'Sure, what use is all that money to me at my time of life? It'll sort the pair of you out, and you'll be taking it with me blessing. Think of it as an anniversary present.'

'No, you could take yourself off, a holiday, maybe.'

'I'll not be needing one of those, although I might treat meself to a new pair of boots.'

The knock at the door surprised them both.

'Now, who would that be?' said Fearghus. 'It's not Nancy.'

'Well, it's not the feckin' fairies. You best find out.'

Fearghus returned and ushered two gentlemen into the kitchen. They stood, side by side and smiled politely as Brendan eyed them with an air of caution.

'Da, these are the two fellas who called earlier, the detectives.'

'Detectives, eh?' said Brendan. 'Well, you best come in, lads, take a seat and tell me exactly what it is you're detecting.'

Molloy raised his hand and declined the invitation.

'D.I. Molloy,' he said, 'and this is D.S. Hanagan. Would you mind if we had a quick word, Mr. McBride?'

'I wouldn't mind at all,' said Brendan, 'but I always find it easier to chat when I'm sitting down. Stops me talking out me arse.'

Molloy grinned as he warmed to the old man.

'If only that would work for me sergeant, here,' he said. 'Unfortunately, he has the ability to spout shite whatever position he's in. Thing is, Mr. McBride, 'tis a bit, private, confidential, like.'

'I'll go out if you like,' said Fearghus, 'I'll take a stroll, just up the...'

'Very considerate of you, sir,' said Hanagan, 'but it won't be necessary. See, we'd like to have a word with the both of you. But, not here.'

'Where then?' said Brendan. 'Will we go into the other room? Sofa's more comfortable, anyway.'

'No, no,' said Molloy. 'I was wondering if you'd mind coming with us, down the station like. Not for long, and we can't force you. It's just that with all the paperwork and stuff it'd make our life a bit easier. Being a bit selfish, I suppose.'

'Well,' said Brendan, 'I've no plans this evening. I'm not one for staying out til midnight, mind, you understand Inspector?'

'Thanks,' said Molloy. 'I appreciate it, really I do. We'll run you back, too, won't take long.'

Fearghus sat with Hanagan, a mug of tea and a copy of the Racing Post in hand while Molloy led Brendan to a small room along the corridor. Plain and simply furnished with one desk, two chairs, a poster of Van Gogh's 'Sunflowers' stuck to the wall, it had a window overlooking the car park. Brendan took a seat and glanced at Molloy inquisitively.

'Are we in the right place?' he asked.

'Sorry?' said Molloy.

'This room, 'tis too cheerful, is it not? For interrogating people, like?'

Molloy grinned.

'Would you rather a cell with bars on the window and a couple of rats for company?' he said.

'I would. It's all about creating the right atmosphere. Ambience, they call it. You'll never get a confession in a room like this.'

'I'll bear it in mind, now…'

'Hold on,' said Brendan.

'Something wrong?'

'The spotlight. You've to shine a spotlight in me face. Have you not done this before?'

Molloy laughed and sat down.

'You know something, Mr. McBride?' he said. 'It's moments like this that make me job worthwhile. Shall we go on?'

'I'm all ears.'

'Right, first things first, can I get you get something to drink? Tea, coffee, a drop of something, maybe?'

'A drop of maybe would be nice,' said Brendan.

Molloy took a bottle of whiskey and a Styrofoam cup from the drawer and set them on the desk.

'Help yourself,' he said. 'But, before you do, one thing. Would you mind if I took your fingerprints? It's just a request, you've no obligation, but it might save time and, no doubt, eliminate you from the inquiry. Then we can stop hassling you.'

'Sure, why not, Inspector, I've nothing to hide, as long as you leave the bottle on the table.'

Brendan wiped the ink from his hands and helped himself to a drink.

'They won't take long to check,' said Molloy. 'In the meantime, no doubt you'll be wondering what all this about.'

'I'd be lying if I said it hadn't crossed me mind.'

'Well, you see, Mr. McBride, there's a fella been killed, murdered, so he was. He, er, he had his throat cut. In his hotel room.'

'We heard about that,' said Brendan. 'In The Blue Haven, was it not? He had a funny name, sounded like a pizza.'

Molloy paused, then offered 'Balducci.'

'That's it.'

'It's not him. This is a different fella.'

'A different one?'

'Name of Reilly.'

'And you think the two murders are related? I suppose they must be, I mean, two murders in the same town within a few...'

'It wasn't here. It was in Waterford.'

Brendan froze, momentarily, long enough for Molloy to notice, and knocked back his whiskey.

'Does that mean something to you, Mr. McBride? Waterford?'

'What? No, why?'

'You seemed shocked.'

'Who wouldn't be? Two fellas killed, it's getting so you can't walk the streets at night.'

'Don't you go worrying yourself, now. It's perfectly safe out there, trust me. This is a one-off, a unique case.'

'I'll take your word for it. So, what has this to do with me and the lad? What do you need to know?'

'Like I say,' said Molloy, 'Reilly had his throat cut. The knife was quite unusual, a farmer's blade, I think you call it, but we tracked it down.'

'Good work, Inspector, that can't have been easy. And you think it's like the one I gave me boy?'

'I'm afraid, Mr. McBride, it is the one you gave your boy. We found Reilly's DNA on it.'

'What?' cried Brendan. 'Well, now, how can that be? What would his DNA be doing on our knife?'

'That's what we're trying to find out.'

'You must be wrong. You must've made a mistake, got them all mixed up or something. It doesn't make sense.'

'Calm yourself, now,' said Molloy. 'We're not pointing the finger at anyone, just trying to get to the bottom of it. Please don't distress yourself, I don't want to upset you.'

'So, you're just checking? I mean, you don't think Fearghus... he wouldn't have, he couldn't, hasn't got it in him.'

'I'm not accusing you, or Fearghus, of anything. Here, take a drink. Could be anything, someone might have borrowed it, picked it up by mistake, that kind of thing. Sure, there's lots of possibilities.'

'If you say so,' said Brendan, draining the cup. 'Will I be staying the night, then? Locked up, surrounded by the stench of urine, sleeping on a blood-stained mattress while the gaoler sits outside me room?'

Molloy smiled and shook his head.

'No, Mr. McBride, I've a better idea. I'll get a Garda to run you home now, while we have a chat with Fearghus. He'll be along soon enough, I promise.'

Fearghus, unable to relax, toyed nervously with his jacket, his face wrinkled with fear and confusion. Hanagan sat back and folded his arms while Molloy did his best to put him at ease.

'It's alright, Fearghus,' he said. ''Tis just a friendly chat, informal, like. You've nothing to worry about. Really.'

Fearghus' eyes darted anxiously between the two of them.

'All the same, it's a bit... I mean... I've never been in trouble before, never...'

'You're not in trouble, honest. Will you take a drink, glass of water? Tea?'

'No, thanks. How's me Da? Are you holding him somewhere?'

Hanagan laughed.

'Fearghus, this isn't Hill Street Blues,' he said reassuringly. 'Your Da's away, probably home by now. We just need to ask a few questions, then you can join him.'

Fearghus sighed with relief.

'Okay, thanks. So, what can I tell you?'

'Do you ever go out much?' asked Molloy? 'You and the wife? Dinner, dancing, that kind of thing?'

'You must be joking!' exclaimed Fearghus. 'After what we've been through, sure, we can barely afford to put food on the table.'

'So, you'll not have been to The Blue Haven, recently?'

'The Blue Haven?' said Fearghus, laughing. 'No, we've never been there, not once, too expensive for the likes of us. The last time we went out, well, we didn't even go out, we were on the way home, we stopped at The Grey Hound for a pint, but that was it, one pint, and that was, oh, three, four months ago, now.'

Molloy took Brendan's cup and poured himself a tot of whiskey.

'Have you taken a trip recently?' he said, without looking up, 'A day out, somewhere away from Kinsale?'

'Have you somewhere in mind?' said Fearghus.

'No, not really, nowhere in...'

'Farthest I've been is to pick up me pigs, half an hour away.'

'So, you've not been to, say, Youghal, maybe, or Dungarven, or Waterford?'

'Sure, now, why would I be going Waterford? We don't know anyone there.'

'How about Sligo?' said Hanagan.

'Sligo?'

'I'll take that as a no, then.'

'Look, I don't know where this is going, but you're troubling me, now. I'd like to go home.'

'No problem,' said Molloy. 'I appreciate you coming down, Fearghus, been most helpful, so you have. We'll get a Garda to drop you home. Oh, one last thing, if it's not too personal, would you happen to have a photo of your wife?'

'Me wife?'

'That's right. Most men carry a photo in their wallet, I just wondered...'

'I have, but why?'

'Just like to put a face to a name,' said Molloy. 'If you don't mind.'

Fearghus took a black and white, passport-size snap from his wallet and handed it over. Molloy's eyes widened as he recognised the mysterious lass from the CCTV footage and passed it to Hanagan. He swallowed hard.

'You're a lucky man, Fearghus,' said Molloy. 'She's very pretty.'

'She is, that.'

'What's her name?'

'Nancy.'

Molloy glanced at Hanagan, the corner of his mouth, raised knowingly.

'Would you... would you happen to know where she is?' he said. 'What time she'll be back?'

'Can't help you, there, I'm afraid. I haven't a clue.'

'You wouldn't be trying to cover for her, now, would you?' asked Hanagan.

'Cover for her? Why? What's she done? What's going on? I told you, I haven't a clue where she is. She stormed off this morning.'

'Stormed off?' said Molloy.

'We had an argument, more a disagreement, really.'

'About what?'

'Babbies,' said Fearghus. 'Having kids.'

'Ah,' said Molloy, 'Sorry. I didn't mean to pry.'

'It's alright. I always thought we'd have a couple of kids, but she seems to have an aversion to them.'

'And you don't know why?'

'No,' said Fearghus. 'Every time I broach the subject, she goes feckin' mental, but she can be moody like that. Has a habit of taking off when she's upset. You might call her unpredictable.'

'Well, now, the thing is, Fearghus,' said Molloy, 'the thing is, we really need to speak to her. There's someone who looks a lot like her who may have done something illegal, and I wouldn't want her being arrested by mistake, you understand?'

'Illegal?' said Fearghus 'Like…'

'I can't say, confidential, like. Will she be home tonight, do you think?'

'At some point. She always comes home. She may be there now.'

'Okay,' said Molloy. 'I need a favour, Fearghus. I'm going to go back to your place, now, to see if she's there, would you mind waiting here for me? I think it might be less stressful for her if she sees you here when we get back. Wouldn't want to worry her, now, would we?'

'Well, alright, then. I suppose that's alright. Can I have a drink now? Same cup is fine.'

'Of course, you can, help yourself. Maybe we could have your fingerprints while you're waiting, too, just for the record, like.'

Molloy, concerned that Brendan may say something to Nancy and scare her off before they arrived, loosened his tie and drew a deep breath in a futile effort to steady his nerves. He rapped the steering wheel as he waited impatiently for Hanagan.

'Sorry, Jack, had to wait for the check on Brendan's prints. I think you'll…'

'Don't worry about those,' said Molloy, as he sped from the car park, 'he has nothing to do with it.'

'What?'

'Neither has Fearghus.'

'I think you might change your mind,' said Hanagan, smugly. 'They've a partial print on the knife, reckon it may match the old fella's.'

'Doesn't mean a thing. He's innocent of any wrong doing.'

'I don't get it! We have the knife, Reilly's DNA and the distinct possibility that old man McBride left his prints all over it. Case closed. Surely?'

'Have you been wearing plugs?' asked Molloy. 'Fearghus's wife is called Nancy, she's the girl from the feckin' CCTV and the knife has Reilly's DNA on it. That is case closed. 'Tis Nancy McBride, or Cathleen Moran we're after. I'll stake me reputation on it.'

'Not much to lose.'

'Careful.'

'Sorry,' said Hanagan. 'I get the feeling we're in for a long night, then?'

'I hope so. Mrs. Molloy's got a Stroganoff on the hob.'

CHAPTER 12

Brendan, unable to relax in the kitchen where the toxic stench of swine manure tainted the air, retired to the living room, clutching the Paddy's and a glass. He stood by the window and stared into the darkness, pondering his encounter with the police, and wondered when Fearghus would return home. He checked his watch and took a sip of whiskey. He was old enough, and wise enough, to know the trip to the station was nothing more than a ruse to get their fingerprints without making a formal arrest. And he could feel, in his bones, that something bad was about to happen. He jumped at the sound of the back door opening.

'Fearghus?' he called, heading for the kitchen. 'Nancy! You're back, and who the hell is this adorable fella?' He dropped to his knees as an incorrigible Labrador accosted him and lavished his face with kisses.

'His name's Bailey,' said Nancy.

'Bailey? And where on earth did you come from, Bailey?'

'I found him, wandering in the lane.'

'Is that so?' said Brendan, suspiciously. 'In the lane? Sure, there's no-one round here owns a dog like this, he must've walked for miles.'

'If you say so.'

Brendan hauled himself up and regarded Nancy with a tilt of the head. Her hair was damp and bedraggled, her boots, caked in mud and her face, with bags under the eyes, as weary as a well-worn shoe.

'Are you alright?' he asked. 'You look a state, so you do. Been crawling through a hedge backwards?'

'I'm grand,' said Nancy. 'Just grand.'

'I'll put the kettle on,' said Brendan. 'So, did you have a nice day? Where have you been?'

'Nowhere special. Just out. Thinking, is all.'

'Thinking, eh? Well, this fella looks hungry to me. Will I give him some food? I think we've a sausage or two in the fridge.'

''Tis your supper,' said Nancy. 'Feed him if you want to go without. Where's Fearghus?'

'Long story,' said Brendan, as he fed the hound and filled a bowl with water. 'You'd best sit down.'

'I'll not sit, just tell me what's happened.'

Brendan sighed, resigned to the fact that, with Nancy in one of her moods, any chance of a rational conversation with his daughter-in-law was lost.

'He's helping the police with their inquiries,' he said morosely.

'What?'

'We both were.'

'What do you mean?'

'The police,' said Brendan. 'Detectives they were. They came calling, earlier this evening. Took us down the station. I'm not long back, meself.'

'What did they want?' said Nancy, growling with frustration.

'They were asking about the knife.'

'The knife? For feck's sake, Brendan, what knife?'

'Fearghus's blade. The one he gave you after the fella in the hotel was killed.'

Nancy fumbled in her pockets and shifted uneasily on her feet, keen to avoid Brendan's penetrating gaze.

'What on earth do they want with that old thing?' she asked, biting her nails.

'They have their reasons, but I think you know that, don't you, Nancy?'

She raised her head and smiled at Brendan. 'And what, exactly, is that supposed to mean?' she said, softly.

'Ah, come now, Nancy, stop the charade, will you. You know what I mean. The night you came back from Waterford, you took the knife from your pocket, it was covered in blood, so it was. Only, it wasn't your blood, was it?'

'Of course it was! I told you, I cut meself.'

'So you did. Thing is, you've no scar. On your hand. That much blood, you'd have a scar, so.'

'It feckin' healed.'

Brendan shook his head in dismay.

''Tis a miracle worthy of Lourdes, if it did,' he said sarcastically.

Scowling, Nancy lowered her arms, her hands rolled into fists.

'What are you accusing me of, Brendan?' she said, clenching her teeth. 'Do you think I killed someone? Is that it? Do you really think…'

'I've given up thinking, lass. As of this evening, I've started praying instead.'

'I'll not stand here and take this abuse from me own father-in-law!' yelled Nancy. 'How dare you accuse me of… your own…'

'I'm accusing no-one, Nancy. I'll stand by you no matter what happens, you know that. I just don't want…'

'Stand by me? So, I'm guilty of something, then? That's what you think, isn't it? You know something, Brendan, I thought you loved me, I thought you cared about me.'

'More than you'll ever know.'

She stared at Brendan, her eyes misting over.

'I'm going for a shower,' she said. 'Then I'm away to see Fearghus.'

The dog, tail wagging, wandered over to Brendan and sat at his feet.

'You know something, Bailey?' said Brendan, patting him on the head. 'I think she could use a cup of tea, calm her down. What do you think? Maybe, she's hungry too, I'll go ask.'

He climbed the stairs and gently tapped the bedroom door.

'Nancy, love?' he said. 'Will I make you a sandwich? Are you hungry?'

With no reply, he inched open the door and called again, the noise from the shower drowning out his voice. The box on the bed caught his eye. Curious, he stepped inside for a closer look.

'Holy Mary, Mother of God,' he mumbled, eyeing the pile of banknotes and a box of Tryptizol lying within the folds of the dress. 'I should've known. I should've feckin' known.'

Glancing at the bathroom door, he carefully pushed aside the wad of notes with his forefinger to reveal a bank card and drew a deep breath as he read the name 'Balducci'. Beside it lay a driver's licence. His stomach turned. He recognised the face, he'd seen it often enough, every day for a decade. It was the name that troubled him.

'Who the hell is Cathleen Moran?' he sighed, as he closed the door behind him.

Nancy, refreshed and relaxed, breezed into the kitchen, her disposition, amiable.

'I made you a tea,' said Brendan. 'Will you have something to eat?'

'Thanks. No,' she said, cheerfully. 'I haven't the time. I'm away to see Fearghus, see if we can't sort this out. Some silly misunderstanding. I'll be…'

'Nancy.'

She stopped in her tracks and turned to face him.

'What?' she said. 'What is it?'

'Don't go,' said Brendan, his voice low and serious.

Nancy flicked her head and regarded him with a curious smirk.

'Sure, I'm only going to town,' she said. 'You'll not miss me, I'll be back before…'

'Don't go,' said Brendan. 'You set one foot in that police station and I promise you, you'll never get out.'

'What are you talking about?' said Nancy.

'You know what I'm talking about. I'll not stand here and argue about it. Just leave, for your own sake Nancy, just leave, and get as far away from here as you can.'

'Are you trying to get rid of me?' she said, giggling.

Brendan could take no more.

'I'm trying to protect you!' he snapped. 'Can't you see that? I'm worried you might…'

'Might what?'

'You might… Nancy, love, you need help, you can't go on…'

She laughed, flung her arms around his shoulders and hugged him tight. 'You're losing the plot, so you are. Must be an age thing.'

'Me?' asked Brendan. 'Losing the plot? Maybe I am.'

* * *

Brendan sat dozing on the sofa while Bailey, stretched out beside him, snored contentedly, his head resting on his lap. The sound of tyres crunching stealthily up the gravel drive woke him with a bark.

'That'll be Fearghus,' said Brendan, as he nudged Bailey to the floor and struggled to his feet. A familiar rap on the door told him otherwise. 'Maybe not.'

Molloy's angst-ridden face wrinkled with an apologetic smile as he stood in the doorway.

'Back so soon?' said Brendan, silhouetted by the light in the hall.

'Apologies, Mr. McBride,' said Molloy. 'I didn't want to disturb you, it's getting late, but I really...'

Brendan peered over his shoulder towards the car.

'Have you forgotten something?' he said.

'What? No, I don't think so.'

'Me son.'

'Ah, no, see, he's down the station, he'll be back soon. Said he'd wait while we popped round to see, to have a word with, Nancy.'

'Nancy?'

'Right. Won't take long, nothing important, really. Is she home yet?'

Brendan rubbed his chin and sighed as though befuddled by the question.

'Well, yes, and then, again, no.'

'I'm confused,' said Molloy.

'Yes, she was here, and no, she isn't, anymore. You've just missed her.'

'Missed her?' said Molloy, exasperated. 'Well, where the devil has she gone? When did she leave?'

'About ten minutes ago.'

'But we passed no-one. There was no-one in the lane.'

'Sure, we don't walk the lane, Inspector, takes too long. We cut across the field, there.'

'Do you know where she went?'

'I do,' said Brendan. 'Your place. She's gone to see Fearghus.'

'I don't believe...'

'Well, when I told her where we'd been this evening, she couldn't wait to get there. Can't blame her for wanting to see her own...'

'Could you not have kept her here?' said Molloy.

'And how was I to know you'd be coming to see her?'

'Fair point,' said Molloy. 'Sorry. Right, thanks, Mr. McBride, I have to go, bit of a hurry, now.'

'Goodnight to you, then. Oh, and don't forget to send me son back, he's quite useful to have about the place.'

Molloy, holding on for dear life, rolled in his seat as Hanagan, driving like a tail-ender at Le Mans, slew the car around the tight, country lanes before leaving it to rest, skewed across the pavement, outside the station. They dashed inside, leaving the doors flapping in their wake. The desk sergeant, startled by their arrival, greeted them with a look of surprise.

'Where's the fire?' he said.

'Where is she?' said Molloy, panting as he caught his breath. 'Did you put her in with McBride?'

'Put who in with McBride?'

'His wife. Nancy. She was on her way here.'

The desk sergeant, perplexed and slightly worried that the messenger may be shot, shook his head and shrugged his shoulders.

'Well, she hasn't arrived. Sure, no-one's come through those doors except the two of you,' he said. 'Not a soul.'

'What? No-one?' said Molloy. 'Short lass, this high, dark hair?'

'Nope,' said the Sergeant.

'Shite. Feckin' shite. What about McBride?'

'Still in the interview room, Sir. McCluskey's outside, just in case.'

Molloy, flustered, paced the floor, scratching the back of his head.

'Right,' he said, waving a finger at Hanagan and the desk sergeant. 'Listen carefully, this is so feckin' important, if you mess up, so help me God, I'll crucify the lot of you. Get a car back up to McBride's place, now. Don't drive the lane, park at the bottom and cut across the field, something may have happened to her.'

'The field?' asked the Desk Sergeant. 'At this time of night, Sir? They'll not see a thing.'

Hanagan, keeping his distance, looked to the floor and smiled.

'I've already got the cross, all I have to do is put your name on it,' said Molloy, scowling. 'Now, do as I say, and quick. Any more of your lip and it'll be a different kind of desk you'll be sitting behind tomorrow. Understand?'

'Sir.'

'I want every available man out looking for her. Call them in, get them out of bed if you have to. She can't have gone far. I want roadside checks, every feckin' road out of Kinsale, and a watch on the buses and the trains and the boats and the airport. Call the taxi firms, see if they've picked anyone up in the last half hour that looks like her. Oh, and get someone up to the bus station in Cork city. She's ahead of us, maybe on her way there. Now, anything else? Yes, so, listen, if she's taken off, she may be using her real name, Cathleen Moran. Got that? Make no mistake, this lass is dangerous, and she's a danger to herself.'

Molloy, already exhausted, turned to Hanagan and lowered his voice.

'I need you to do something for me, right away,' he said.

'Anything, Jack, name it.'

'I hate to do it, but, I want you to call Anglesea Street, fill them in on everything. We need all the help we can get if we're to find her.'

'Not a problem, I'll do it now. One thing, I've just seen this.'

'What is it?' said Molloy.

'Match for the prints on the knife, you were right, it isn't the old fella.'

'Wouldn't matter if they were.'

'It's Fearghus. Thumb print, on the handle, perfect match.'

'So?'

'Well,' said Hanagan, hesitating, 'I just thought, if push came to shove, we have the knife, the prints, the…'

'I'll pretend I didn't hear that,' said Molloy. 'You should know better by now. I want you to hold him anyway, we've at least a day left. Once you've called HQ, get in there and speak to him.'

'What about?'

'Ask him about Nancy's habits, who her friends are, where she usually goes when she takes off, but do it nicely, right? He's a decent lad, don't scare him.'

CHAPTER 13

The sun, still low and unhindered by cloud, dazzled against a clear, blue sky. Bailey, enthralled by the weaners, snorting and squealing in the mud, sat obediently by the fence, wagging his tail as Brendan, bleary eyed from a restless night, mucked out the pen.

'Have you ever seen a sausage on legs?' he asked the dog, closing the gate.

Bailey barked enthusiastically, as though he understood every word.

'Let's have some breakfast,' said Brendan. ''Tis a fine day ahead, we don't want to waste it.'

Were it not for the bacon sizzling, the toaster whirring, the kettle boiling and the radio blaring, Brendan would have heard the telephone ring the first time, or the second. As it was, he'd barely sat down when it rang again. Taking no chances, he carried his plate to the hall to answer it, aware that Bailey, having wolfed down his own breakfast, had his eye on it too.

'Sergeant Hanagan?' he said. ''Tis not yet 7 o'clock, could you not sleep?'

It was hard to determine whether the laughter down the line was genuine or not.

'Hope I didn't wake you,' said Hanagan.

'That's almost funny,' said Brendan. 'Now, where's me son?'

Hanagan explained that Fearghus, whilst not being charged with any offence, had kindly agreed to remain at the station to help with the inquiry, in particular, the whereabouts of his wife. Brendan almost dropped his plate.

'What do you mean, missing?' he said, flabbergasted. 'I thought she was with you! She went to see you last night, to see Fearghus.'

'She didn't arrive,' said Hanagan. 'We're looking for her now.'

'Didn't arrive? But you were ten minutes behind her, and driving. Sure, you'd have caught her up.'

'That's what we thought,' said Hanagan.

'May the Lord have mercy. And you didn't think to telephone, to let me know?'

Hanagan floundered.

'No, I mean, I should have, I know, it was an oversight, we were so wrapped up, you know, trying to find her, like.'

The pause in the conversation had Hanagan squirming with embarrassment.

'Have you told Fearghus?' asked Brendan, quietly. 'Does he know?'

'He does, Mr. McBride.'

'Is he alright?'

'He's holding up, 'tis quite a shock, but I think he's fine, we're looking after him. We've been out all night, searching, like. We're doing our best, Mr. McBride, honest.'

'Sure, I can't believe someone could just disappear between here and the station,' said Brendan. 'It's a twenty minute walk. Will I come? Do you need the help? I've a dog, he could maybe sniff her out.'

'That won't be necessary, we've a few ourselves. Best you stay home, in case she comes back, may be just a worry over nothing, so.'

Brendan sighed and tossed Bailey a rasher of bacon.

'Alright,' he said. 'If you think that's best. And Fearghus, when will he be back?'

'Not long. This afternoon, I dare say. Sure, he's been a great help.'

'You'll telephone me if you hear anything?'

'Rest assured, Mr. McBride, we will, that. I promise.'

Brendan, Bailey in tow, returned to the kitchen, turned off the radio and sat at the table, toying with his food.

'Nothing like cold toast to set you up for the day,' he said, offering it to the hound.

His mind wandered as he slurped his tea, cradling the mug in both hands. An image of Fearghus and Nancy sitting opposite him, laughing and full of expectation for the future, brought a wistful smile to his face. They were young, carefree, a picture of contentment. If only he'd known then, what he knew now. If only he'd recognised the storm that raged inside her. Hanagan's words, reverberating round his head, brought him to with a jolt, '*Best you stay home, in case she comes back*'.

'Wait here,' he said to Bailey, as he rushed upstairs.

He stood outside the bedroom door and listened for a moment before optimistically pushing it open. It was just as she'd left it. The wedding gown, still rumpled, spilled from the box on the bed, but the cash was gone, as was everything else.

Back in the kitchen, Bailey, sitting on his chair, was clearing the breakfast plate of crumbs.

'Well,' sighed Brendan, as he sat beside the dog. 'I've a feeling we'll not be cooking for three for a while. I was planning on going to Dublin today, but that will have to wait, I mean, I can't leave you alone, can I? Christ knows what you'll eat. And anyway, that Hanagan fella told us to wait here, just in case, so we may as well do something useful. No point in wallowing, is there? What say we take care of the rubbish Fearghus has cleared from the barn, then we'll take a walk up the woods?'

* * *

Hanagan, recognising the now familiar jaded expression on his boss's face, reached for the kettle as Molloy, looking haggard, shuffled into the office and collapsed in his chair. He stretched, yawned and rubbed the stubble on his chin, sneering as it rasped against his hand. Hanagan handed him a mug of tea.

'Rough night on the sofa?' he said.

'I'm getting used to it,' said Molloy. 'If I could just get a couple of inches taken off me legs, I'd be fine.'

Hanagan smiled and pointed casually at his jacket.

'You've something on your shoulder... looks like a pigeon...'

Molloy peered down and scraped the crusty blemish with his fingernail.

'Stroganoff,' he said. 'The rest is on the wall. How's Fearghus?'

'Fine, so,' said Hanagan. 'I think he's sleeping. Doesn't look like he wants to go home.'

'Can't blame the lad. Make sure he gets a decent breakfast, anything he wants. So, what's up? You look edgy. Has something occurred?'

'Well, I didn't want to rush you, you look done in, but...'

'It's alright, Sergeant, I can cope. What is it?'

Hanagan drew a breath.

'The lads from Anglesea Street, they're on their way,'

'Thought me ears were burning...'

'I'm to tell you not to... they want us off the case. They said...'

'Don't worry what they said, Sergeant, I'll not be retiring yet. You and me, we're going to see this through to the bitter end. With or without them. What?'

'There's something else.'

'And what would that be?' said Molloy.

'I think we've got another,' said Hanagan.

Molloy dropped his head in his hands and rubbed his eyes.

'Another? There'll be no-one left in this town if it carries on like this,' he said, holding up his mug. 'I don't care how early it is, stick a drop of something in that, will you, anything, paraffin if you have to.'

He took a sip and sighed.

'Come on then, who, what, where, and why didn't you call me?'

'I did,' said Hanagan. 'You'd already left. Come so, we should go, before the pips get here.'

'Where to?'

'Castlepark. McCluskey's there now. The landlady at The Dock telephoned not half an hour ago, in a state so she was. She's the first point of contact for anyone renting one of those holiday homes. Says the fella who looks after them, fella called Harry Malone, didn't show up this morning.'

'And that's unusual?' said Molloy.

'Apparently,' said Hanagan. 'Says you can set your watch by him.'

'Surely the Garda can take of that?'

'He did, and you'll not like what he's found.'

McCluskey, at least a foot shorter than the overly-inquisitive landlady from pub, was doing his utmost to prevent her from entering Malone's house, ducking and diving like a featherweight in an effort to obscure her view. It was the only thing, thus far, to bring a smile to Molloy's face.

'Etna!' he said, laughing, as he trudged towards them.

'Jack Molloy! Didn't expect to see you here.'

''Tis a job for the professionals, this.'

'So, they sent you instead.'

'Still as sharp as butter knife, I see. How have you been?'

'Just grand,' said Etna, smiling coyly. 'And yourself?'

'Can't complain. Much. Look, we'll have a chat, so, in a moment or two. I have to take a look in here, first. Will you wait? I'll not be long.'

Molloy inspected the lock, hanging from the door by a single screw.

'Oh, that was me, Sir,' said McCluskey proudly. 'I had to break it down on account that there was no answer when we came.'

Molloy lowered his voice and leaned towards him.

'Have you called anyone else?' he asked.

'No, Sir. He was obviously, you know, when I found him, so there was no need for an ambulance and Sergeant Hanagan said he'd call forensics cos I knew it wasn't... he didn't... he didn't die of natural causes.'

'You're sure about that?' said Molloy.

'Oh, sure as anything,' said McCluskey, 'just wait til you see the mess inside.'

Molloy eased open the door with the side of his foot and waited for Hanagan before stepping inside.

'Did you call forensics?' he said.

'Aye, and Tom. He'll be along, shortly.'

Hanagan eyed the living area with its wood burner, oil lanterns and ample sofa, like a magpie in a jewellery store.

'Do you think this place'll come on the market soon?' he said, smiling broadly.

'What?'

'I could live here, really. It has character, charm, and it's quite cosy. Probably go for a song, now, what with, you know...'

Molloy, perusing the shelves, sighed with disbelief.

'He liked his poetry,' he said. 'Clever man. Stove's still warm, and...'

He paused at the sight of Malone, crumpled on the floor, naked save for his shorts, his arms, now rigid, bent behind his back.

'No, no, no,' he said, shaking his head. 'She doesn't hold back, does she? For the love of God, why… I mean, a single jab with the knife would've done the job. Sure, she didn't have to make a meal of it.'

Hanagan squatted beside the body. 'Maybe that's how she gets her kicks,' he wondered aloud. 'Judging by the bruising to his wrists, I'd say he was tied up. Oh, and strangled too, by the looks of it.'

'Then why carve him up as well? I mean, was that really necessary?' said Molloy. 'And with a bread knife?'

'Maybe she didn't like the sandwich, she left that behind. Obviously had a bit of a tussle too, unless it's the cleaner's day off.'

Molloy wandered to the bedroom.

'I'd say the tussle started here,' he said. 'The bed's a mess.'

'Wonder who the boy is?" said Hanagan, gazing at the shattered picture frame. 'Son? Nephew?'

'We'll do a trace once they've dusted it. Wouldn't like to be the one to tell him if it is.'

McKinley appeared, his gangly frame wavering in the doorway.

'Jack, you're making a habit of this,' he said. 'I'm beginning to think you're some kind of Jonah.'

Molloy turned and smiled.

'Well, I live with a whale, so you're half right. Good to see you, Tom, and not before time. He's through there.'

McKinley stood over the body, pulled on his gloves and waved aside a fly.

'When did you find him?' he asked, crouching down.

'About an hour ago,' said Molloy. 'Can you give me something quick, Tom? I can't afford to wait for an official report.'

'No problem, Jack. Ten minutes.'

Molloy, grabbing Hanagan by the elbow, pointed to the sofa on their way out.

'What?' said Hanagan.

'Dog bowl.'

'So?'

'Where's the dog?'

* * *

Etna O'Brien, widow and proprietor of the only bar on the peninsula, clasped her hands behind her back, smiled flirtatiously at Molloy and swaggered towards him, her skirt flapping in the breeze.

'You're looking well, Jack,' she said, fingering his lapel, 'if a little tired.'

'Goes with the job, Etna. I must say, you're looking as fresh as ever.'

'I'm always fresh, Jack,' she said, with a wink. 'So, how's Mrs… still breathing fire?'

'Only on the weekdays. Rest of the time she's casting spells.'

'Well, you know where to come when she's polishing her broom. It can get awful lonely after closing time.'

'I'll bear it in mind,' said Molloy with a smirk. 'So, tell me Etna, what brought you here?'

'Why, the Garda, of course. Had to show him the way.'

'That's not what I…'

'I'm teasing you, Jack,' she said. 'There's a couple staying in one of the houses. Full of the old airs and graces, so they are. Anyway, they knocked me door this morning, early this morning, crying on about a leaking tap. I mean, a tap for Chrissakes, not like it was the end of the world. Anyway, I got fed up, told them to feck off and drove up here to fetch Harry. I knocked the door but there was no answer, so I went back to the pub and called the Garda, and here we are.'

'When did you see him last?' said Molloy.

'Yesterday. He finished lunchtime, gave me the keys and off he went. Nice looking fella, Harry, and a kinder man you'll never meet. Do anything for anyone. I've often dreamt about him sorting out me U-bend.'

Molloy, hands in pockets, kicked the turf and chuckled.

'You don't change, do you Etna?' he said. 'Was anyone asking after him, last night, in the pub? Anyone you didn't recognise, maybe?'

'No, just the same old faces.'

'And he seemed alright? In himself, like, not troubled by anything?'

'No, he was his usual, happy, handsome self,' said Etna. 'So, what's happened, then? Has he been robbed or something?'

Molloy winced and regarded Etna with a look of sympathy.

'No, he's not been robbed,' he said softly. 'I'm afraid he's, he's no longer with us.'

'What? Oh, sweet Lord, you don't mean…' she said, crossing herself.

'And we have to treat this as a crime scene for now, til we know what happened.'

'Crime scene? You mean…'

'It's just procedure. Probably just a heart attack, but we have to be sure. Come so,' said Molloy, passing her a handkerchief, 'wait in the car and I'll run you back.'

McKinley emerged, breathed in a lungful of fresh, salty air and snapped off his gloves.

'Well, Jack,' he said, 'naturally, I'll have to do a thorough investigation, but there's a couple of things of which we can be certain.'

'Go on, Tom,' said Molloy. 'Anything could help.'

'In a nutshell, the bruising to the neck, ligature of some kind.'

'Rope?'

'No, wrong shape,' said McKinley. 'Whatever went around his neck was about an inch wide, inch and a quarter, maybe, and flat, like a belt. I'd say it was the buckle that did most of the damage, right here, just above the Adam's apple. And he's bruising to the wrists as well, but that's different, that could've been a rope, nylon rope, perhaps. I'll know more later.'

'Do you think,' said Molloy, hesitating with mild embarrassment, 'do you think it could've been something… sexual? You hear of people getting, you know, tied up, round the neck and hands, when they…'

McKinley grinned like a mortician at a massacre.

'I've not only heard of it, Jack, I've seen it, too. And, yes, it's possible there may have been an element of sadomasochism about the encounter, but that's not what killed him.'

'I figured that one out meself, Tom.'

'Although, looking at the trauma round the eyes, and the severity of the bruising to the neck, I'd say he came close. May even have passed out.'

'Can you give me a time of death?'

'Not long, ten, twelve hours, I'd say, give or take.'

'Thanks Tom,' said Molloy. 'You've been a great help, so. Pint on me when you drop by.'

Hanagan pulled up outside The Dock. Molloy leapt from his seat and opened the door for Etna.

'Are you okay?' he asked.

'Sure, I'll be fine. It's just so, unexpected, that's all. He was so young.'

'Have yourself a brandy, and get some cover, don't be working the bar, now. You've had a shock.'

'Thanks, Jack. Oh, one more thing,' she said, anxiously, 'Bailey.'

'Bailey?' said Molloy. 'Who's Bailey?'

'Harry's dog. Oh, he's a lovely fella, he is, young thing, so full of life. He'll be distraught, I couldn't bear to think of him wandering off somewhere, no food, no…'

'Don't you go worrying yourself, now. We'll keep an eye out. Promise.'

She leaned in and gave him a peck on the cheek.

'You're a sweet man, Jack,' she said. 'And don't forget what I said. I can cast the odd spell, too, you know.'

They crawled across the bridge, Hanagan staring pensively through the windscreen, his mind elsewhere.

'Are we running out of petrol?' said Molloy. 'Sure, the ducks are moving faster than we are.'

'Sorry,' said Hanagan, stepping on the accelerator. 'I've been thinking. Remember that fella from up the way, Dermot something or other, the one we found in the woods a while back?'

'I do. Sad state of affairs, that was,' said Molloy. 'What about him?'

'Well, thing is, Jack, I've been over it in me head a hundred times and I can't help but think, he didn't have to do it. I mean, the fella was loaded...'

'I wouldn't say that,' said Molloy. 'Sure, he had a pension or two, and some savings, but...'

'Point is, just because his herd had the old mad cow thing, he needn't have given up, he could've carried on.'

'Ah, he wasn't thinking straight, Sergeant, things got on top of him. When you're that worried about your business, your farm, your family, all that responsibility, your mind gets, clouded. Stressed out, so he was.'

'Even so...'

'I know, if only he'd talked to someone, he could've...'

'No,' said Hanagan. 'I mean, it doesn't add up. His wife took care of the finances, she knew what they were worth, and she'd have told him.'

'You're not suggesting his wife...'

'No, not her, but something's not sitting right. I'm just not convinced he took his own life.'

'What?'

'I'm beginning to wonder if he was the first.'

'The first?' said Molloy. 'The first what? The first... Oh, I see where you're going with this, now. You mean the first, as in, before Balducci?'

'Exactly.'

Molloy sat back and pondered the notion, sucking his teeth and sighing heavily as he recalled the case in his mind.

'You know how much paperwork this involves, if we re-open the case?' he said. 'You know how much flak we'll get from headquarters? You know we may even have to exhume the body?'

Hanagan nodded.

'Right, so. You're on. We'll take a look this afternoon. If we still have our jobs.'

Hanagan glanced at Molloy and smiled.

'Hold on!' he said, slamming on the brakes. 'McBride.'

'McBride?' said Molloy, cursing as he fastened his seat belt. 'I wish you'd make your mind up, I thought we were talking about Dermot.'

'When I spoke to McBride, and told him Nancy was missing, he asked if he could help, said he could bring the dog, use it to follow her scent.'

'Don't be daft, only trained sniffer dogs can... hold on, just a minute, the McBrides don't have a dog.'

* * *

The rubbish, piled high in a shallow ditch, was nothing that wouldn't waste away of its own accord, thought Brendan, but, if Fearghus wanted it out, he must have his reasons. So out it would go. Decaying timber posts and festering fence panels mingled with an old gate, lengths of tired rope, rotting potato sacks, picture frames and all manner of discarded, cardboard boxes, tea chests, telephone directories and even an aged carpet infested with weeds.

He fetched a Jerry can from the barn and, shooing Bailey a safe distance away, walked around the heap, dousing it with petrol as he went, barely noticing the gentle breeze blowing from the south. Kneeling down, he struck a match, tossed it onto the pile and watched, entranced, as the flames danced and licked the timber into submission. It crackled and popped, like a bowlful of breakfast cereal, before settling to a steady blaze. Brendan stepped forward, as close as he dare, reached into his pocket and pulled out a bundle of banknotes. Leaning forward, he threw them into the belly of the fire, followed by a bank card and, finally, an old driving licence. He watched with relief as the flames engulfed the sheets of plastic and turned them into melting, bubbling pieces beyond history. Bailey grew restless, perturbed by something untoward, something ethereal. He raised his head and whimpered softly as the putrid stench of burning flesh floated through the air.

CHAPTER 14

It was Bailey who alerted Brendan to their arrival. He turned at his bark to see Molloy and Hanagan lumbering across the field, their gait, slow, their shoulders, sagging. He hauled himself up and stood to greet them.

'Gentlemen,' he said. 'How's the doctor?'

Hanagan frowned and regarded him quizzically.

'Doctor?' he asked. 'Sorry, Mr. McBride, I don't…'

'I thought you went to see him, about the old Alzheimer's.'

'Alzheimer's?'

'You've forgotten me son. Again.'

'Ah, right, yes. No, we came from the other side, you see. We'll fetch him soon, though, soon as we get back.'

'We came to see this fine looking fella,' said Molloy, crouching to stroke the dog. 'I don't recall you having a dog, Mr. McBride.'

'No, no, we didn't,' said Brendan. 'Well, not til now. He's what you might call a new acquisition.'

'I don't mean to interrupt,' said Hanagan, wearing a pained expression, 'but if you don't mind me asking, Mr. McBride, what the feck is that smell?'

'Smell?' said Brendan. 'Oh, that'll be Fearghus's sausages.'

'What?'

'The pigs, or rather, the pig shite.'

'Smells like burning… no, rotting…'

'Ah, 'tis nature at her best,' said Brendan. 'The old pig shite, see, is a mixture of all kinds of horrible things, like ammonia and cadaverine and sulphides. Smells like a pork chop, gone off, wouldn't you say? A big, pork chop.'

'I wouldn't know,' said Molloy. 'But I'll be glad when you get the sheep back. Anyway, like I was saying, about the dog, would he happen to be called Bailey, by any chance?'

'Sure, he would that, and how would you know?' asked Brendan. 'Did you find the owner?'

'So, you knew he was lost, then?'

'I did.'

'Would you mind me asking how you came about him?' said Molloy.

'Nancy. She brought him last night.'

Molloy glanced furtively at Hanagan.

'Nancy? Is that so?' he said. 'And, did she happen to say where she got him?'

'Said he was wandering down the lane, there. I said he must've walked for miles cos there's only a couple of dogs, hereabouts, and they're collies.'

'Well,' said Hanagan. 'He certainly stretched his legs, that's for sure. He's from Castlepark.'

'Castlepark? Explains why he nearly took me fingers off when I fed him. Ravenous, he was.'

'You don't think Nancy… I mean, you wouldn't happen to know if she was over that way, yesterday, by any chance?'

'Sure, now why would she be in Castlepark? There's nothing there but the pub and a handful of houses'

'Just thought I'd ask.'

'Well, you never know with Nancy, I'll ask her, when she... So, I suppose you've come for Bailey, to take him back, like. Repatriate him.'

'Not exactly,' said Molloy. 'As of now, he's homeless. I'm afraid the owner's passed away.'

Brendan shook his head in dismay.

'Passed away?' he said, crossing himself. 'That is a shame. Well, 'tis no wonder the fella ran off, then. Must've been traumatised. Will you be sending him to a home, or one of those rescue shelters?'

'No, no, if I'm honest,' said Molloy, 'I haven't even thought about it but, I mean, if you fancy... if you're happy to, why don't you keep him?'

Brendan cracked a smile and gave Bailey a hefty pat on the shoulder.

'Me? Really? Sure, I'd love to,' he said. 'You know, I'm quite fond of the fella, already. Be good company, so he will.'

'Well, that's sorted then.'

Brendan cleared his throat with a subtle cough and lowered his voice.

'On a more serious matter,' he said, 'I don't suppose you've found our Nancy, then?'

Molloy shook his head, despondently.

'No, Mr. McBride,' he sighed. 'I'm afraid not, not yet, but we've not given up. We're still looking. I was going to ask you the same question, if you'd heard anything, a phone call, maybe?'

'Not a word, Inspector,' said Brendan. 'Nothing. But it's not unusual. Nancy's a flighty lass, a will-o'-the- wisp, if you will. I'm sure she'll come when she's ready, this evening perhaps.'

Brendan watched them leave.

'Then again,' he muttered, 'she may not come at all.'

CHAPTER 15

Fearghus trod tentatively down the dark, shadowless hallway. The house was cold and foreboding, inexplicably empty, as though it had lost its soul. He surveyed the kitchen, an empty mug and a tumbler lay in the sink, a breakfast plate, smeared with brown sauce, sat on the drainer. The only sound came from the dripping tap, plinking as it struck the glass. The back door was open. The fuggy reek of a well-stoked bonfire drifted on the air. Outside, the pigs were snuffling through the grass and the mud, happy with their lot. Brendan, he noticed, had company.

'Da!' he yelled, heading for the barn.

Bailey let out an almighty bark and bounded towards him.

'You're back!' said Brendan. 'About time, too. Meet your new housemate. He'll eat anything the pigs won't.'

'Where the feck did he come from?'

'Nancy brought him last night,' said Brendan. 'Ran away from home, he did...'

'Nancy?' said Fearghus.

Brendan dropped his shoulders and let out a heavy sigh.

'Aye, Nancy. Pitched up with the hound last night, took a shower then left ten minutes later to see yourself. That was the last...' Brendan grabbed Fearghus by the shoulders. 'How are you feeling, son? Did the peelers say anything? Any word?'

Fearghus hung his head.

'Not yet. It doesn't make sense, Da, she always comes back. She never stays out.'

'Now, don't you go fretting yourself, son,' said Brendan. 'It's early days. Come, let's go inside.'

'No. I think I need to keep busy, get some air, take me mind of it.'

'Nonsense. You don't realise just how much of a shock you've had, you and me both, what with Nancy and the police and all their questions. Come inside, you need to rest.'

'And do what? Sit in that house and twiddle me thumbs? No,' said Fearghus, staring at the fire. 'No. Here. I'll give you a hand, we'll...'

'No! No, no, no. Leave that, 'tis fine. It'll burn for hours yet. Come so, we'll put the kettle on.'

Bailey, sprawled across the floor like an over-sized draught excluder, watched from the corner of his eye as Brendan poured the tea.

'I know you're worried, lad, we all are,' he said. 'Christ knows, I've barely slept meself, but if you carry on moping like this, you're going to get yourself nowhere, fast. Try to be a little more positive, a little, optimistic.'

'Easier said than done,' replied Fearghus. 'What if... What if something's happened to her?'

'Something happen to Nancy?' said Brendan, grinning in an attempt to lift spirits. 'Sure, you know as well as I do, she could take down any fella, with her tongue mainly. She can look after herself.'

'She can, that,' said Fearghus, smiling. 'But it doesn't stop me worrying. I wouldn't be without her. Despite her faults. Be like losing an arm.'

'Life goes on,' said Brendan. 'You've got to…'

'What would be the point of going on without her? Really? Tell me that. Everything I've done here, I've done for her. For us. I don't know if I want it without her.'

Brendan eyed his son earnestly.

'I felt the same when your mother passed,' he said, quietly. 'Sure it killed me too, but you have to retain a sense of worth, some dignity, some self-respect, and carry on, carry on so's she'd be proud of you. Do you understand?'

Fearghus rubbed his eyes.

'I think so,' he said. 'But it doesn't…'

'Just pretend she's away, on her holidays, like,' said Brendan. 'Just for now. And imagine the surprise you'll get when she turns up, unannounced. Look, you've done well with the pigs, you're getting yourself out of a hole, used your initiative. Don't throw it all away just because the lass has stopped out for a night or two.'

'You're right,' said Fearghus, taking the ring from his pocket and placing it on the mantle. 'Thanks, Da. Well, I could use a shower, feel filthy from kipping in that cell, and the fella with the boar is coming tomorrow, I'll have to check the big girl's alright.'

Brendan, having endured a torturous night haunted by images of blood-stained steel, rose at first light. He slipped from the house, Bailey behind him, and carefully raked over the charred detritus from the fire. He tossed aside the blackened gate hinges, a couple of coils of fencing wire, half a dozen metal brackets, and gazed, repentantly, at the few remaining pieces of grey, calcified bone. He recognised something that used to be a hip, another fragment, the remnants of a shoulder. Two rows of teeth, once glistening and bright, sat scorched in what was left of a skull. The bone, surprisingly, shattered with ease, each blow of the hammer reducing it to splintered shards and bite-size chips. He buried the chaff and raked over the soil with the ashes.

'Nice spot for a rose bush,' he muttered to himself. 'You always were fond of the old roses, weren't you?'

Fearghus, barefooted and clad only in his pyjama bottoms, padded into the kitchen, drawn from his bed by the scent of sizzling bacon and burnt toast.

'I told you, you needed to rest,' said Brendan. 'How're you feeling?'

'Better, so. And starving. You'll not appreciate your own bed til you've kipped on a flea-bitten mattress, that's for sure.'

'Here. Get that down you,' said Brendan, passing him a plate. 'And don't go working yourself into the ground today. You're to take things easy, do you understand?'

'Yes, Da,' said Fearghus, sarcastically.

'I've cleared the fire. Ground's fine, so no need to worry about that.'

'Already? Christ, what time is it?'

'Doesn't matter,' said Brendan. 'Now, once you've eaten that and made yourself half decent, you can deal with the fella and his boar. After that, will you take Bailey a walk for me. He'll need a good run, so, then feed him. Not before.'

'Of course, but... are you going somewhere?'

'I am,' said Brendan. 'I'll not be long. I'm away to Dublin with me coins. Hoping that fella likes writing cheques with lots of zeros on the end.'

* * *

The sun, having dropped below a blanket of cloud, was shimmering on the horizon as Brendan returned. He watched the boar, penned off from the sow, pacing the fence like an inmate in an open prison anticipating visiting day. The sow, unimpressed, retired to the ark with her brood.

The house was silent. Bailey, panting with excitement, leapt on him as he entered the kitchen. Exhausted from the trip, he called to Fearghus, grabbed a couple of glasses and a bottle of Paddy's and shuffled into the living room. His son cut a lonely figure, hunched in semi-darkness on the edge of the sofa, scrutinising the ring.

'If you're going to sit there, cogitating,' said Brendan, slamming the bottle on the table, 'wallowing in grief and feeling sorry for yourself, I'll take meself off and find someone cheerful to be with.'

'I'm fine, so,' said Fearghus, glumly. 'Just, you know...'

'No, I don't know. What have you done today? Apart from take delivery of that porker out the back?'

'I... not much. I miss her Da. Already. I don't feel right. I need to hear her shouting at me over something, something so trivial it drives me mad. I want to see her scowl like she married the spawn of the devil. I just want...'

''Tis only natural, lad,' said Brendan, relenting. 'I don't mean to give you a hard time, but it's for your own good.'

'It's the not knowing thing. That's the worst part. Not knowing if...'

'Well,' said Brendan, raising his voice and filling the glasses. 'I've something to cheer you up. Here.'

He opened his wallet, unfolded a large cheque and handed it over.

'What?' said Fearghus, aghast at the figures staring back at him.

'I had the fella put your name on it. It's all yours.'

'But... 58,000? That's feckin' insane! For a few rusty coins?'

'Now you're sounding like Nancy.'

'58,000?'

'I know,' said Brendan. 'Crafty beggar knocked me down me down on a couple of them, said they weren't up to scratch.'

'I don't believe it.'

'Nor did I, feckin' chancer, but, what's a few hundred between friends? A toast. To new beginnings.'

Fearghus smiled and raised his glass.

'To new beginnings,' he said softly. 'Right. First, we'll decorate the bedroom, the whole house even, could do with a bit of sprucing up, wouldn't you say? She'd like that, to come back and see the place all clean and fresh. Will I get her a new outfit, too? A new coat, maybe? And a couple of dresses? Oh, and I was thinking, the top field, let's forget the crops. I mean, it's clear of the old Scrapie, we should get the sheep back. Ah, sure, she loved those sheep, especially the lambing, she...'

Fearghus's voice grew faint and distant as Brendan, paying no heed, stared solemnly out of the window, sipping his whiskey, his mind ticking like a bomb.

'Fearghus,' he muttered.

'...And maybe we should take a holiday, all three of us. Sure, that'd be grand, would it not? We should do that first, before we get the sheep, we could go to...'

'Fearghus!' snapped Brendan. 'Will you hold your tongue! I've something to tell you.'

The room fell silent. Fearghus stood stock still, almost quivering with shock. He hadn't heard his father raise his voice in twelve years, not since the passing of his mother.

'I can't stand here and listen to this anymore,' said Brendan. 'Listen to you getting carried away with your hopes and your dreams. 'Tisn't fair, on any of us.'

'What?' pleaded Fearghus. 'What isn't fair?'

'I can't keep it to meself any longer, the burden is...'

'What? What burden? Are you ill? Is that it? Is it the old cancer or something?'

Brendan filled his glass to the brim, took a large swig and leaned against the table.

'It's not the cancer, son. It's Nancy.'

'Nancy?'

'Sit down,' he said, sighing heavily. 'Did you know Nancy had... problems?'

'Problems?' said Fearghus.

'Health problems. Mental health problems.'

Fearghus fell into the sofa.

'Is this a wind up? Are you leading me on?'

'She was suffering from depression,' said Brendan. 'Manic depression. She was on the old medication, so she was. That's why she was so… changeable. Moody…'

'Ah, you're talking bollocks, Da! Sure, I would've known, she's me feckin' wife!'

'I only found out meself, by accident, like, when…'

'Found out?' said Fearghus. 'What? Did she tell you herself? Were the two of you conspiring behind me back? Is that it?'

'No, no, no. Just listen. I found the pills, the empty packet of pills, in the kitchen, so I took …'

'That means nothing! They could've come from anywhere, sure, blown in off the lane, even, she could've picked them up.'

'… I took them to the doctor. He told me what they were. She had a big box of them, enough for a month or two, stashed away, upstairs. I saw them when she brought the hound.'

Fearghus's eyes widened as he stood and glared at his father.

'So, you know, don't you?' he said.

'Know what?' said Brendan.

'Where she is. Where she's gone. She told you, didn't she?'

Brendan shook his head.

'No, son. She did not. I swear to God, I wish she had. There's something else.'

Fearghus sat down again.

'The police.'

'What about them?'

'They're not just looking for Nancy because she's… disappeared.'

'What then? Come on, Da, for Christ's sake, just spit it out.'

'They think, they think she killed the fella in the hotel,' said Brendan, 'The Blue Haven.'

'What?'

'And another, in Waterford.'

'Oh, that's it! I've heard it all, now!' said Fearghus.

'Can't you see, Fearghus? Jesus, that's why they asked if you'd been to Waterford! His name was Reilly. He came from Sligo.'

Fearghus's face froze.

'That's right. Sligo,' said Brendan. 'Ring any bells?'

Fearghus, hands shaking, filled his glass and knocked back the whiskey before taking another.

'So, you're saying me wife, Nancy, Nancy is feckin' murderer? Are you insane? Are you all feckin' insane? She…'

'Remember when she went to Waterford? When she pulled the blade from her pocket? Said she cut herself? Did you see a scar on her hand?'

Fearghus fell silent.

'Fearghus!' yelled Brendan. 'You sleep with the feckin' woman! Did you not even see a plaster on her hand?'

'No. No, I did not.'

'That's why they wanted the blade. It wasn't her blood on it. It was Reilly's.'

'Holy Mary, Mother of God. What has she…'

'Come, so. Sit with me. 'Tis a lot to take in.'

'What do we do?' said Fearghus, his eyes welling up as he paced the floor. 'I don't… will we call the peelers? I need… I need to go, I need to get out.'

'Fearghus! Son!' called Brendan after him. 'Where're you going? Come back and…'

Bailey barked as the door slammed, jumped on the sofa and held aloft a consoling paw.

* * *

Feeling as crumpled as his shirt, Brendan rose from another restless night, pulled the curtains and shielded his eyes from the rising sun. He called to Fearghus with the offer of tea and toast, put the kettle on the hob and wandered outside with Bailey. The boar was waiting patiently by the fence, staking out the ark, his eyes glinting with eager anticipation. The sound of tyres crunching slowly up the gravel drive drew Brendan from the pen, his heart skipped at the sight of Molloy and Hanagan emerging from the car.

'What is it?' called over, quickening his pace as he approached them. 'You look like you've seen a ghost, the pair of you. Is it Nancy?'

Molloy, exhibiting a distinct lack of jocularity, buttoned his jacket. 'I'm afraid we found another body,' he said. 'And no, Mr. McBride, it's not Nancy.'

'Not Nancy?' said Brendan. 'That's a relief. I mean, that sounds like a terrible thing to say, I didn't mean…'

His words tailed off as he realised what he'd heard, his brow furrowed with bewilderment and his shoulders twitched as a chill ran the length of his spine.

'Another body? he said quietly. 'So… so, the killer, the fella who's been murdering all these folk, he's still on the loose?'

'Maybe, so,' said Molloy.

Brendan blinked, rapidly, the colour drained from his cheeks and tiny beads of perspiration gathered on his forehead as his heart began to thump and pound against his ribs.

'Jesus, Mary and Joseph,' he mumbled, his hands clammy and cold. 'What have I done?'

'Are you alright, Mr. McBride?' said Hanagan. 'You've gone quite pale.'

'She didn't do it. After all that, she didn't… I was trying to help, I thought it was for the best…'

'Sorry,' said Hanagan, smiling politely. 'You'll have to speak up, we can't hear you.'

'What?'

'We were wondering, would you mind coming with us? Won't take long.'

A look of terror crossed Brendan's face.

'It's alright,' said Hanagan, 'we're not arresting you or nothing. You've done nothing wrong.'

Brendan's eyes darted between the detectives as he frantically ran his fingers through his hair.

'Right, so,' he said nervously. 'Of course, of course I'll come. Just let me turn off the kettle. Oh, Bailey. Will I bring Bailey? I can't leave him here, alone.'

'Ah, sure, no problem. He can sit in the back with yourself.'

Brendan, his face contorted with grief, eased himself into the rear seat, made the sign of the cross and began rambling incoherently, 'Forgive me Father, for I have sinned. Hail Mary, full of grace…'

'You'll recognise the place, be like a home from home, so it will,' said Molloy as he led them to the interview room.

The 'Sunflowers' were not as Brendan remembered them, they appeared somehow faded and dour, the chair harder, the walls, greyer.

'Have a seat,' said Hanagan. 'We'll not keep you long, I'll fetch you a cup of something, see if I can't find a bowl and a bone for old Bailey, too.'

An air of depression filled the office. Hanagan, looking forlorn, perched himself on the edge of his desk and folded his arms while Molloy, scratching the back of his neck, sighed and groaned.

'It'll be a shock for the old fella,' he said. 'I just hope it doesn't…'

'I know Jack,' said Hanagan. 'I was thinking the same thing but what choice do we have?'

'I know, I know, it's just, sometimes… For feck's sake, why does it always happen to the wrong people?'

'Will you tell him or shall I?'

'Ah, it makes no odds. Come so, there's no easy way of telling a father his only son has killed himself.'

EPILOGUE

Brendan. Brendan McBride. Like I said before, he's half the man he used to be. Troubled, so he is. Some folk are blessed, see, they have good fortune showered upon them, whilst others, well, others like Brendan, they get the opposite. It was bad enough losing his daughter-in-law but to lose his son as well? So soon after? No-one deserves that, unless of course…

It's amazing what the police can do these days, with all that science and technology and those fancy tests you see on the television. Sure, they can take a body from the ground, a body that's lain there fifty years or more, and tell you exactly what killed them, the colour of their hair, and probably what they had for breakfast, too. They did that over at Brendan's place. 'Twas the day serendipity smiled on the Police. A fluke, it was, a complete and utter stroke of luck, a case of being in the right place at the right time. Couldn't believe it, meself, when I heard. Took some convincing, I can you tell you that, and even now…

Anyway, after the funeral, see, Fearghus's funeral, a couple of days later it was, this inspector fella turned up at Brendan's, called himself Molloy, just to see how he was doing, how he was coping, like. He'd asked after the dog, Bailey, thinking he had gone away or was out a walk, maybe, because he didn't come to greet him and Bailey always barked and ran to greet the visitors, he was good like that. Brendan's mind was elsewhere. He thought that maybe Bailey was in the kitchen, so they went looking for him. He wasn't far.

Safe enough, he was, out by the barn. Digging and chewing, as a dog does. Paid no heed, even when they called to him. And that's when they found Nancy. Or rather, what was left of her. Brendan all but collapsed on the spot. She'd been under his nose the whole time. Can you imagine how that must've felt? Would've turned me stomach, I'm sure of that. So, the inspector, he scraped around in the hole Bailey had dug, just with his hands, and he found something unusual. Not what you'd expect to find in a hole in the ground. It was a tooth. A human tooth. Actually, there were lots of them, some still in the jaw. And there were bits of bone and stuff, too. Well, I don't need to tell you what happened next. The whole place was ablaze with the blue, flashing lights and men in white suits and face masks, digging and dusting and scraping.

Turns out this DNA stuff they got from the teeth, it matched the DNA they found at The Blue Haven Hotel, where that American fella was killed. And it matched the stuff they found at some place in Waterford. And, it matched the DNA they found over at young Harry Malone's place. There was no doubt about it. The bits they found in the hole used to be Nancy McBride. And when she was whole, Nancy McBride had murdered those three fellas. Possibly four. There's talk she may have seen off young Dermot too.

'Nancy?' I thought. You couldn't make it up. 'Twas hard to believe. She was so kind, so polite, so, so small. How could anyone so small kill those big men? Then we heard about her health problems. Problems with the old mind, like, and as if that wasn't enough, turns out she wasn't Nancy at all, but a girl from Kilkenny, some lass called Cathleen. Could've knocked me down with a feather, I mean, that's the kind of thing that happens in the films, not in feckin' Kinsale. Ten years she kept that a secret, ten years. Not even her husband knew.

She was convicted, posthumously, of course, but she got a decent burial, we all made sure of that. She may have been guilty of murder, but she couldn't be blamed, now, could she? Not with the problems she had.

So, you'd have thought they'd have left it there, the police, I mean Brendan had been through enough, had he not? But no. One question remained. One loose end that needed tying up. If Nancy had killed those fellas, then who the feck killed Nancy? It didn't take long for them to find out. Some lass from far away, London, I think, turned up the following day. I can't say what you call her, 'tis a long word, longer than any I've ever heard, but she was clever. Oh, she took a long, hard look at the ground, studied the roots and the growth patterns of the plants, the amount of insects and things crawling around, the condition of the teeth and the bones. She even took samples of the soil. Then she locked herself with away with her microscopes and things and a couple of days later, she was able to tell the police when the bits, I mean, the remains, were buried there. To within a day. Sure, you'd have to be clever to do a job like that.

It was about that time they called for a doctor, for Brendan. Not for his physical state, sure. He's always been strong as an ox, that man. No, it was 'to assess his mind', they said. Seemed like he was losing it. He'd insisted it was him who'd killed Nancy. Like a dog with a bone, he was, kept on and on, told them he'd strangled her, with his bare hands, did it the night she found Bailey wandering in the lane, the same night Fearghus had spent with the Police down the station. He said he knew what she'd done, that she had to be stopped, for her own sake, for everyone's sake. The police listened, and the doctor listened, and they didn't believe him. Not a word. Said his story didn't add up, so they gave him some pills. Lots of them. He's not been the same since.

Turns out it was the clever lass who said he couldn't have done it. Based on her conclusions, she was convinced he would've been in Dublin the day the hole was dug. And they had plenty of proof that he was, indeed, in Dublin. They went through all the evidence, too, all the results from the tests, and came to the only possible conclusion. It knocked me for a six. It was bad enough being told young Nancy was a murderer, but Fearghus too? I still don't buy it, but he's not here to defend himself, is he? I knew Fearghus like I know Brendan, and he was besotted, in love, so he was. He couldn't have done it, wouldn't have done it, not to his beloved Nancy. Fair play to Brendan for protecting his son like that. I'd have done the same, I think, but according to the courts, there was no doubt about it, young Fearghus murdered his wife and he simply couldn't live with the guilt. Too much stress, they said. Too much stress.

If you enjoyed this book, please let others know by leaving a quick review on Amazon. Also, if you spot anything untoward in the paperback, get in touch. We strive for the best quality and appreciate reader feedback.

editor@thebookfolks.com

www.thebookfolks.com

Other titles by Pete Brassett:

SHE
AVARICE
ENMITY
KISS THE GIRLS
PRAYER FOR THE DYING
THE WILDER SIDE OF CHAOS
BROWN BREAD
YELLOW MAN
CLAM CHOWDER AT LAFAYETTE AND
SPRING